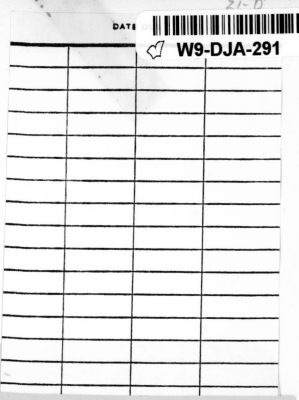

The Heart's Highest Hurdle

The Heart's Highest Hurdle

A Novel of the Olympics

by

DOROTHY C. HASKIN

ZONDERVAN PUBLISHING HOUSE

GRAND RAPIDS   MICHIGAN

CONTENTS

PART I

KNOX "God will not look you over for medals, degrees or diplomas, but for scars."

Elbert Hubbard

1

"The important thing in the Olympic Games is not to win, but to take part. The essential thing is not to have conquered, but to have fought well."

Pierre de Coubertin,
Founder of the Modern Olympiads

Knox Taylor stood in front of the bureau of his bedroom and, with elation, stared at his Olympic decathlon medal. It stood for the two great moments of his life, his winning it and the fact that within an hour he was going to offer it to the girl who already had his heart. He snapped shut the case and slipped it into the pocket of his sport jacket. "Wish me success!"

Vince Redl, his hefty body clad in green sports shirt and slacks, was lying on the lower bunk bed. With envy in his small, brown eyes, he said, "Why wish you success? You've already got everything you want. She'd be a fool to turn down the champ."

"I'm not so sure." Knox picked up an enlarged snapshot of a slim girl in a sweater and skirt. Shortly after his return from Rome he had met her at church, and one Sunday brought her home to dinner. Afterwards they'd gone for a walk and he'd snapped her picture. A breeze had blown her dark hair away from her face, and her eyes smiled warmly. He said, "It isn't only that she has looks but she knows what the score is. Only of late when I'm with her, I feel like I'm missing the mark."

Vince swung around, sitting on the edge of the bed. "You'll get her just as you've gotten everything else. You've always out-run, out-thrown, out-jumped everyone, including me."

"You did your best and that's what counts." But Knox knew how disappointed Vince was. Shot-put champion of the United States, with a throw of 60.3, Vince had hoped to be Olympic champion. Instead, the title had been taken with a 60.5 throw by a Canadian entry. To the crowd and officials, Vince had taken defeat with proper sportsmanship, but in his room he had sobbed. Knox knew, for he and Vince had been close friends in Rome and at UCLA. And so Vince had gratefully accepted the invitation to visit the Taylors over the Christmas holidays.

Knox picked up Alison's gift-wrapped package of bone China teacups and saucers he had bought abroad. "I'm slipping out the back way so as not to get involved in trimming the Christmas tree. Tell Mom if she asks."

"It's a deal."

Knox smiled at his friend, then stepped lightly down the hall, out the back door, into his convertible. As he swung over to the freeway and headed toward Los Angeles, he thought of the grueling years of training it had taken to win his Olympic medal. His father, Bull Taylor, had been All American tackle in his college days and was a high school coach. Bull wanted Knox to go in for football, but track had proven to be his natural.

When he was a high school freshman he entered the decathlon events at a track meet in Fresno, California. When the points were totaled he knew the ecstacy of winning, and set the Olympic championship as his goal.

Bull had snorted with pride and set up a regime for Knox that made the Egyptian taskmasters look like amateurs. He and Knox ate, slept and talked nothing but the training of Knox's strong, lithe body. Even his younger brother Stuart was a team member, carrying the shot or discus or retaping the pole. Knox came out of his whirl of dust only long enough to keep up his grades. They, as far as Bull was concerned, were an old-fashioned must!

When Knox went to UCLA, on his locker door in the basement of the men's gym he taped the words, "Inches make the champion," and, "Work is the price of success." Every afternoon after classes he crossed the street from UCLA's main building to the athletic field to gain an inch on this event, a second on another.

He lived through the suspense of the trials, making the Olympic team.

In Rome, Knox and Vince shared a room in the Olympic village. Over eight thousand athletes, trainers and managers from sixty-eight nations were quartered there, while Bull lived at a hotel within walking distance.

On the opening day, August twenty-fifth, one hundred thousand spectators crowded the stadium with the flags of the competing nations flying high.

The next few days were crowded with heartbreaking competition between men in short pants with long numbers. Vince and others lost to inch winners. When Knox lined up for the hundred meter dash, he was beyond nerves, trained to a pitch. He ran the race with his head bobbing in rhythmic jerks, his spikes scratching forward, finishing in 10.4, one second off his best record! The crowd cheered and even Coach Keane slapped him on the back.

The broad jump was next. With arms stretched forward, muscles rippling, he made 24.6. Then came the shot-put. The sixteen pound shot seemed light in his hands. He watched it float through the air, and though he made 50½, the contender from Australia bettered him. *But,* he thought, *it's the over-all points that win.*

He gauged his speed and height correctly, making the high jump at 6'4". An inner half-felt weariness made his four hundred run 0:48.9, not his best.

That night, Knox, Bull and Vince gathered in the fellows' room and discussed the days' records. They agreed that Knox had a chance to win. It was a crazy feeling, half excitement, half deep satisfaction.

The next morning as Knox laced his track shoes, he prayed, *Lord, this is it. Help me do my best!* The spectators cheered the team onto the field. Exhilarated, he ran the high hurdles in fourteen flat.

When he picked up the discus it felt light in his hand. His stance too was tops, but he made only 154.11. Again the contender from Australia bettered him, throwing the discus 156.

It took seemingly hours for the pole vault event. He watched his competitors' tries, ever higher and higher. When his turn came, he carefully checked the tape of the long pole. Then with exact timing, he stuck the pole in the ground, swung both his legs up, and his body cleared the shaft at 12′9½. The shouts of the crowd became a roar. Coach Keane congratulated him and hurried him into his sweat shirt and loose pants.

In the afternoon the field was lined up again. He threw the javelin 195 feet, his best record! Only one event was left, the 1,500 meter race. When it was called, he paced even until the last two laps, then gave a powerful spurt forward and finished in 5.03 — a total of 7,990 points!

Everyone in the stadium went wild. Knox stood in the center of the hubbub, feeling as if he wanted to vomit. He was like a top that had stopped spinning, and could only stand there, letting the cameramen take his picture, letting the coach do the talking.

Off the field, Bull had a cable all written out to send his wife. Of all the honor given Knox, that which pleased him most was his father's pride.

Honor continued to be heaped upon him on his return to the states, and to UCLA. And yet with all the excitement of meetings and dinners had been the undercurrent of his romance with Alison. If only his achievements were enough to please her. But there was a side to Alison that he never quite understood. She spent her spare time teaching craft to underprivileged children at Olvera House near the Plaza in Los Angeles.

He was on his way there to see her. *And I hope to take her away from it. Not that those kids don't need help, but I want her to have more time for me!*

He turned off the freeway near the Union Station, parked and walked across the Plaza. Olvera Street was festive with lights and packed with last-minute Christmas shoppers. Its Mexican quaintness contrasted sharply to the modern Olvera House, located just north of it. Knox went down the six steps to the basement level, into a side door that led to a hallway next to the chapel. He could hear a children's choir rehearsing, "The cattle are lowing, The Baby awakes, But little Lord Jesus, No crying He makes." Knox thought, *Christmas is the happiest time of the year!*

He paused in front of an open door. In the room, Alison, in full blue skirt and paint-daubed smock, was sitting on a table. With a look of warm intimacy, she leaned toward the young man standing in front of her. Knox could see only his back, tall and lean, the basketball type.

Alison reached up and touched the man's face, her blue eyes glowing. A feeling of jealousy and apprehension filled Knox. He instinctively touched the pocket where he had put his medal and somehow he knew, *I'm not offering her enough!*

2

"Success is full of promise till men get it, and then it is as a last year's nest, from which the bird has flown."

Henry W. Beecher

Knox stepped into the craft room with its cupboard-lined walls and long tables covered with strips of linoleum, stubby knives, paint-piled palettes, rollers, inks and stacks of newspapers. Alison took her hand from the young man's face and smiled self-consciously at Knox.

"Am I intruding?"

"Of course not. Ben, this is Knox Taylor. Knox, this is Ben Moore, one of the workers here."

"Alison has told me about you." Ben put out his hand. His firm grip and plain, friendly face demanded Knox's admiration.

"We were talking about one of the boys who's missing from choir rehearsal," Alison said. "Joe Mendoza. He comes from a home with plenty of children and no money. He has been picked up for stealing two or three times, but because he'd done it to help his mother, the judge put him on probation and had our superintendent, Mr. Buchanan, contact him."

"Buchanan turned him over to me," Ben admitted in an accusing tone of voice, "so what happened is my fault. I talked over Joe's head, expecting too much of him. And tonight his sister told me she thinks he's working for Orci."

"Orci's the scum of the earth! He's a pusher."

"A what?"

14

"Pusher. That means he sells dope," Alison explained. "That is, we think he does. He comes from a poor family, was a prize fighter and now claims to be a car salesman. But he doesn't sell any cars and he does have plenty of money. We find that if one of the boys becomes friendly with him, sooner or later he's arrested as an addict. It's terrible!"

"You mean this stuff we read in the papers is for real?" Knox asked, shocked at Alison's being mixed up in dope and crime.

"I've got to find Joe. It's been great meeting you, Mr. Taylor, and if you'll excuse me ------" Without waiting for a reply, Ben hurried out of the room.

"I hope he finds this Joe." Knox glanced after Ben, realizing how sorry he must feel to have failed the boy.

"He will, if it's at all possible. Ben's completely consecrated."

"Sure," Knox said, forgetting Ben in his delight in being with Alison again. He held out the blue-wrapped gift package. "Merry Christmas!"

"For me?"

"Unwrap it, see if you like it," he answered, anxious.

"It looks too perfect to spoil." Her deft fingers untied the gold bow and placed it on the table beside her. Then taking the paper and the cover off the box, she reached into the layers of crushed tissue paper, lifted up a cup and saucer.

Knox again thought it the most beautiful he had ever seen. The saucer was black enamel with a gold edge and the cup was black with a gold handle, with four exquisite pink roses inside.

"They're perfect!" She said in a low hesitant voice.

"I hoped you'd like them. And, Alison, I've something else I'd like to give you." He drew in his breath knowing *This is the big moment*. He reached in his pocket for the box with his medals, snapped up the lid, and held it out.

Alison pushed some scraps of linoleum to one side, put her Christmas gift on the table, and took the smaller box. "It's your Olympic medal! I couldn't take it!"

"You could, if we were engaged," he insisted eagerly.

She edged back, holding out the medal. "I couldn't, Knox, I'm sorry, but I couldn't."

"Why?" Hurt and confused, he slipped the medal in his coat pocket. "Ever since I've known you, we've more or less gone steady. You knew how I felt about you."

"I suppose I did. And I thought a great deal of you. Only marriage has to be more than emotion. We have to share interests. What do you expect to do with your life?"

"I expect to be a coach, like Dad."

"That's a good work."

"But not good enough for you!"

"No, I want a man who is completely consecrated."

"Like this Ben! Let's have the guided tour."

"Mind if I finish this block while I'm talking? It's for a little girl who is making a special Christmas card for her mother." She stood up, picked up a brayer and rolled it back and forth in the blue paint on a glass palette.

"Go ahead," he said, wishing he could do something also. Action, any kind of action, would be easier than standing there, listening to childish voices sing, "Joy to the World!" while Alison took all the joy out of his world.

She rolled the brayer back and forth on the linoleum block. "I admire you, Knox. You're good-looking and always doing little things to please a girl. For a while I thought I wanted to spend my life with you, but ------" She picked up the block, measured carefully with her eye and set it ink-side down on a square of white paper. "I met Ben. He's so consecrated."

"You said that before!"

"But he is. He devotes hours with the boys, discussing their problems."

"But not always a success! He said himself that he expected too much of this Joe."

"Perhaps that is Ben's fault; he expects too much of others, of himself and of me." She lifted the block and tossed it to one side. "Try to understand him! His background is different from ours. Our families are average Christians, but Ben's are consecrated."

"There you go again!"

"I mean his father wanted to be a missionary but the board

wouldn't accept him because of Mrs. Moore's health, so they deliberately moved to a poor section of town, and turned their home into a mission. Not the skid row type, but a sort of church in the home. Ben's never known anything but Christian service."

"He had to go to school, didn't he?"

"They sent him to Calvin Academy."

"I've heard of it. Tops in Protestant day schools. Gramps wanted me to go there but Dad said it didn't have a strong enough sports program."

"Ben was on the honor roll and got a scholarship to Wheaton College. That's Christian, too. Now he's going to seminary and teaches Bible here. I attend his classes when I can and ----" Her eyes shone. "He has something!"

"He must have!" The gall of disappointment was eating his heart.

"We're going to be married after graduation and go to Mexico where he'll work among the Indians, reducing one of their languages to writing."

"But, Alison, think of the inconveniences of a life like that. No electricity. Probably not even running water."

"There will be sacrifices, but that's the way Ben is, expecting everyone to live his highest." She clasped her hands together and pressed them against her breast.

He stared at her long fingers, paint-stained, but otherwise bare. "You don't have a ring."

"Ben took the money he would have spent for the ring and gave it to the American Bible Society as an engagement present for me," she answered with a radiant smile.

"I can't offer him competition. All I could offer you would be a garbage disposal unit and a two-car garage." He glanced at his gift of fragile bone China cups. *Now I see why she was confused by my gift.* "They won't fit into your mud hut."

She picked up a cup and held it carefully. "I shall take them with me to Mexico City for special occasions. I appreciate your love and hope you find exactly the right girl."

"Thanks," he said, because there was nothing else to say.

A different tune floated into the room as the children began singing, "O little town of Bethlehem, how still we see thee lie!"

Knox said, "I'd better be going."

"You do understand, don't you?"

"I'm not good at understanding tonight!"

"I don't want to hurt you. I ----" Her blue eyes clouded.

"Don't! I want you to be happy." With a numb feeling he walked out of the room, down the hall, onto the street. As he headed toward his car, each store window blazed with a tree trimmed with lights. But there was no Christmas joy in his heart as he sped back to Santa Ana. His thoughts churned over and over again, *What has Ben got that I haven't? What's the use of being champion if you can't have the girl you love?*

Home again, he slipped quietly through the kitchen, into the darkness of his own room, where he flung himself on the lower bunk bed. He lay there, brooding, when the door opened and closed. Vince snapped on the light, "What gives?"

"I just don't score!"

Vince walked to the bed. "Don't tell me she was crazy enough to turn you down!"

Knox turned over and stared at the slats of the upper bunk. "She said I wasn't consecrated."

Vince swore. Knox glanced at him in surprise. He seldom heard Vince swear. The other fellows, but not Vince. "Don't ever be that!"

"What's wrong with it?"

Vince squinted his small brown eyes. "That's what my dad is."

Knox suddenly realized that Vince seldom talked about his father. He knew that he was a radio preacher in Canada, but that was all.

"All that martyr-complex stuff is just a way of being a hero in your own eyes. I know. Dad moved to Radio Island when I was four. It had only a small rundown radio station on it and a couple of buildings. Dad promoted the station until he is heard around the world. But he had no time for me, or Mom. He didn't have time to take her to the hospital until it was too late. With her gone, I ran wild on the island, getting a little schooling when one of his assistants took pity on me. Now that I'm down here, except for having Lyle, the bookkeeper, send me checks, Dad doesn't know I exist. Knox, don't ever be a saint."

Knox stared at the strip of blue blanket tucked under the upper mattress. Alison's preference for the man ready to sacrifice her and himself for the Lord had opened up a new aspect to him, but Vince only confused him. Upset, he answered, "Tonight I don't even know the score!"

3

"If the nose of Cleopatra had been a little shorter,
it would have changed the history of the world."
Pascal

Knox and Vince stood on the sidewalk of the Rose Parade formation area, watching the floats line up. Their beauty was the culmination of years and months of planning. Contestants had begun their planning before last year's trophy even needed polishing. As soon as the theme of the parade — Famous Firsts — had been announced, the designing had begun and orders had been placed for flowers.

The first step in the construction had been the selection of a stripped-down chassis, consisting of four wheels and an engine. Sometime in October or November the frames, intricate designs of steel or wood, were welded to the chassis. Over this was placed chicken wire, sprayed with plastic coating. Three days ago, the workers had begun gluing the flowers in position, beginning with the hardier species, such as the chrysanthemums and anthuriums. The more delicate flowers such as the roses, carnations and orchids had been placed in individual vials of water and wired in place. The last flower was attached by midnight and the floats had been moved to the formation area on Orange Grove Avenue, from Ellis to California Street.

Knox, with Vince and the other members of the Olympic track team, would ride the Bruin's float. It consisted of a large platform of yellow mums on which the athletes would stand, and around the border, lettered in pansies, was "Hail to the Champ." At the back of the float stood a giant bear of yellow mums.

A short man in a raincoat came up to Knox and Vince, and cocking his head to one side, said, "Beauty, isn't she! Wouldn't be surprised if she were the most beautiful of all the floats I've seen in all the sixteen years I've been working on 'em. There are twenty million mums on this year's floats and this one has her share."

"We'll soon spoil its looks," Vince pulled a stale joke.

"You boys riding her? Then you must be two of the Olympic team. I'm Rosey Saunders."

"I'm Knox Taylor."

Rosey shook hands with him and asked, "You're decathlon champion, aren't you? Won with a total of 7,990 points, didn't you?"

Knox nodded.

"I'm Vince Redl. Can we ditch these raincoats someplace?"

"Inside the bear. You'll find a trap on its side." Rosey sighed. "I can't understand it, of all the three hundred and sixty-five days in the year, on the one that should be sunny, it has to drizzle." He glanced up at the murky sky. "But it will clear up. It always does. Come on and meet the queen and her court. That's her float."

"Lead me to her," Vince said. Knox and Vince followed Rosey to the float in front of theirs. It was comprised of three circular tiered platforms, covered with pink roses and purple stocks and on the third tier was a crown of yellow mums.

"There's a mere forty thousand roses on this float, but there's the most beautiful part of it." Rosey pointed to seven lovely girls, wearing clear plastic raincoats over their wide evening gowns. The girl with the crown on her golden hair wore a white dress and the six princesses wore rose-colored gowns.

Rosey, Knox and Vince walked up to the queen. Rosey said, "I wouldn't be surprised if you were the most beautiful queen I've seen in all the sixteen years I've been working on this parade."

The queen gave him a delightful smile, as if it were the very first time anyone had ever said she was beautiful.

"Here's a couple of champs who want to meet you. Queen Joan VandenBerg, allow me to present Knox Taylor, Olympic decathlon champion, 7,990 points, and Vince Redl, UCLA shotput champion, best distance — 60.3."

"I'm happy to meet you," Joan said.

"And allow me to present you to her court," Rosey waved toward the other girls. "Cathy Anderson, Marilyn Omstead, Peggy Carter, Constance Dyer, Belinda Jones, and Laura Davis."

Knox had the feeling that he was running hurdles as Rosey skipped over name after name and he knew he wouldn't remember which girl was which.

"If you want more details, our golden-haired queen lives in Pasadena, is five-feet-four and weighs one-hundred and-ten pounds.

"You know all the important records!" Vince's eyes swept Joan up and down.

"Please, Mr. Saunders, don't," Joan said.

Being queen hasn't turned her head! She's actually embarrassed! Knox thought.

"I always aim to please the queen, so I won't give any more statistics. Now, if you'll excuse me, I want to see how the cameras are lining up." He went toward the intersection of Orange Grove and Ellis, where TV crews were getting their cameras and lights set up.

Knox nodded, busy thinking that Joan was truly a queen with her short blonde curls, hazel eyes, and tiny waistline.

"Who cares what's upstairs with a stairway like that!" Vince's grin included all of the girls. "Those judges sure know how to pick!"

"And out of fifteen hundred girls," one princess quickly reminded.

"Are they going to let you wear those raincoats on the float?" Knox asked.

"No," Joan answered. "But Rosey says it will clear up, that it always does."

"Sure."

"What'll you wear?"

"Track shorts and varsity sweaters. Don't worry about us, we're used to it, but you-----"

"We're not as bad off as we look." She stepped close to

Knox and he caught a whiff of sweet fragrance. "We have on long winter underwear, and come, I'll show you something."

Knox helped her onto the float and they walked across the beds of pink roses and white mums to the third tier. She stepped into her golden crown, with its double arch and laughed as she pointed, "See, Rosey has a charcoal heater for me. He says in all the years he's worked with queens, he's done his best by them."

"That won't keep you too warm!"

"It really doesn't matter. I only want to be the best possible queen, so Mom will be proud of me."

"She will be!"

"You're going to the game this afternoon?"

"Vince and I will be there."

"So will I, but I have to sit in the queen's place, with my court."

"It'll be a good game." He waited, but she didn't say anything else, so he walked back to the edge of the float and jumped off. Then he reached up, and catching her by the waist, swung her to the street.

"You're strong!"

"Just training, that's for sure."

Joan, the princesses, Knox and Vince talked of the chances of the sun shining, how many people would line the streets to see the parade, and who would win the afternoon's game. Knox noticed that the other team members had boarded their float and said, "We'd better get back. I've enjoyed meeting you girls."

"I second the motion," Vince said. He and Knox walked toward their float. "When a girl's as beautiful as the queen, who cares if the sink is stacked!"

"You've got her wrong. I thing she looks even more spiritual than Alison. Alison is practical, while Joan looks as if she lived at number nine Cloud Avenue."

"That's a blonde for you! Either she looks hard or out of this world. I thought you were carrying the well-known torch for Alison. Let me see, how long have you been down in the basement? A mere week and one day, and already, a pretty face and you're off again."

"Don't get me wrong! I think the queen scores but I'm not interested in her, or any girl right now."

"That's good news to me, because I'd like to look at the merchandise a little closer. Today she's queen, but next week the reign is over and she may want to live a little."

Back at their float, they ditched their raincoats and took their places. Knox at the front, Vince and Lincoln Morrow, Negro discus thrower, on one side; Stan Collier, the sprinter, and Cook McCall, pole vault champion, on the other side. The fellows waited, shivering in the cold air.

At a signal from Rosey the parade started, the five trumpeters leading the way. True to Rosey's prediction, the sun shone wanly. The Long Beach Mounted Police clattered into position, each of the thirty-two riders carrying a large silk American flag. Then came the cars with the Grand Marshal, President of the Rose Tournament, and the Mayor, followed by the Pasadena City College Lancers' Band, official Tournament of Roses musical unit.

Joan took off her raincoat, put it on the floor and stood up. Knox shouted, "You look cold!"

She pointed to the stove with a smile but Knox knew, *That'll only keep her feet warm.*

Rosey signaled the driver of the queen's flat, and he started up Orange Grove Avenue. Two drivers were hidden in the framework of each float. Regardless of the weather, they were hot and uncomfortable, and had to steer through a peep-hole in the flowers. The queen's float inched toward Colorado Boulevard.

Rosey signaled the Bruin's float, and Knox felt it begin to move under him. When he passed the TV cameras, he smiled, knowing, *Many of my friends are watching.* His float passed the special reviewers' stand, where his family had been waiting since before dawn. They waved gaily at him and he waved back.

The float turned east on Colorado Boulevard, going ten miles an hour. Knox marveled at the rows of people who lined each side of the sidewalk, ten to twelve deep. Many of them had been there since before midnight, bringing their pillows, blankets and umbrellas, squatting on the curb so they would have the best view. An estimated fifty thousand were expected to see it, either in person, on TV or newsreels. He passed the corner where the ambulance and receiving station were set up, for each year some people fainted from strain and exhaustion.

He had heard that there were sixty floats, twenty bands, two hundred thoroughbred horses, and over twelve hundred people marching or riding in the parade. *It's wonderful to be a part of all this!*

"Hi, Champ," a boy on the sidewalk yelled.

That's me! The other fellows were national champs or Olympic contenders, but he was Olympic champion. *People cheer me, yet I don't mean enough to Alison. It's a crazy mixed-up world!*

A puff of smoke drifted up from the float in front of him. He stared as another large puff whirled into the air. *It's that stove! The float's afire.* He stepped forward. Joan looked toward him, frightened. A cloud of smoke covered her face. Knox jumped off his float, the impact of the pavement making his feet smart. He half-stumbled forward a couple of steps, then sprinted toward the queen's float.

He sprang upward, landing half-sprawling on the float, and climbed up the rose-covered slope. By now the smoke was rising in waves. Someone had sounded an alarm and Knox could hear the sound of a siren of an emergency truck coming toward them. Joan huddled to one side of the crown. The float lurched to a stop. People left the sidewalk, surging toward the float. Mounted policemen rode back and forth, holding the people back. Knox ripped up the smoking cotton matting and flung it far into the street.

The other princesses hurried toward the crown, calling, "What's wrong?"

Knox studied the quietly burning stove, deciding that the motion of the float had knocked a piece of charcoal out of it, but with the matting gone, nothing else could catch fire. "Just a little fire, but it's out."

"Thank you, Knox, I was so frightened." Joan put her small, cold hand on his forearm and smiled wistfully.

"Now you're safe! Tell the driver to let me jump off and then to go on, or we'll break up the parade."

Joan leaned toward the speaker concealed among the mums. "We had a little fire up here, but Knox Taylor, from the float behind us, put it out. If you'll wait a minute until he gets off, then we can go on."

The princesses went back to their places, waving at the crowd. Knox, thankful for the training that had enabled him to get from one float to another in split-second timing, climbed down the slope of red roses and jumped to the ground. The mounted police urged the crowd back to the sidewalk, clearing a path for Knox to his own float. Vince and the other fellows crowded around him.

"It was nothing," Knox said. "I knew the queen had a heater up there in the crown so when I saw the smoke, I realized it had set the float afire."

They went back to their float. Knox leaned over, and called to the driver, "It's okay. Go ahead."

"You sure get to be a hero in all the right places."

"But with the wrong girl."

4

"The ability to make right decisions largely determines
our success or failure in life."

Norman Vincent Peale

One nice thing about being champion, Knox decided, was
that offers came to him. Though it was several months until he
graduated, he had several offers. One day, shortly after the Rose
Parade, he dropped onto the divan beside his father and said. "I
want to talk to you about the offers I've got."

"Don't take any of them!"

"Why not?"

"You can do better. After all, you're a champion. Cash in
on it. Get the best offer you can. Someone will break your record
and then he'll get the offers."

"But shouldn't I take the best of these three?"

"They're only high schools. Wait for a college or university."

"You usually know the score."

The phone rang in the hall. Lelia Taylor answered it and
called, "It's for you, Knox."

He went into the hall and put the receiver on his shoulder.
"Hello."

"Is this Knox Taylor?"

"Speaking." He couldn't place the voice.

"This is Joan VandenBerg."

Who's she? Then, he remembered, "The queen?"

"Yes. I wanted to thank you for coming to my rescue. It
would have been awful if my dress had caught fire. It was flimsy
material, you know."

27

"It was all in a day's work."

"It was wonderful," she insisted and continued thanking him until Knox was embarrassed. He had acted by instinct and the girl was too grateful! *What can I do to stop her talking?* With sudden inspiration, he asked, "If you're so grateful, how about a date?"

"I could just do that. That is, if I'm free. What did you have in mind?"

He thought wildly of the places he'd taken Alison. "I think there's a concert at the Philharmonic tomorrow night. How about it, if I can get tickets? Suppose I call you back?"

"All right," she agreed, and gave him her number.

"Thanks," and he found himself squeezing in a date with Joan along with moving back to Pi Lambda Phi Fraternity House and heading toward graduation.

His dad proved to be right about his receiving offers to join college coaching staffs. An independent college in Texas wanted him, a small state college in Washington, and then UCLA offered him a place on the staff. Bull ordered, "Take that one! You won't get better. And you'll score both for yourself and the university."

"Sure," Knox agreed. The next day he told Coach Keane that he would accept the post.

He wondered what Joan would think of his coming job so he had a second date with her, taking her to a drive-in, telling her the news. Her green-flecked eyes shone and she exclaimed, "How wonderful!"

Before he left her, he found himself making another date. And when he told Vince, he showed such an interest in Joan that loyalty prompted him to try to get Vince a solo date. Joan refused, but suggested bringing her sister, Sharon, for Vince. Knox told Vince, who agreed. "So she's the fussy kind! Bring on the sister, I'll buy."

Sharon proved to be a lacquered edition of Joan, with golden hair too perfectly set, lips too bright a shade of carmine, and long tapering fingernails. She was a combination secretary and assistant to Cutler Bronson, Pasadena interior decorator. When she went along, she had a knack of wanting to go to the highest-priced place mentioned, until the dates became almost too expensive for Knox.

He preferred the more quiet drive plus drive-in dates with Joan. She gave him the hero treatment, seeming to think anything he did was perfect. She even changed to his church. But for all her admiration, he had an uneasy feeling. *I ought to be doing something bigger with my life. Alison as much as said I was selfish.*

One Sunday evening he and Vince went to the young people's meeting at Grace Church. In the lower auditorium they found seats beside Joan and Sharon. Cliff Jones was leading singing and, as Knox sang, "Brighten the corner where you are," he glanced at the front platform. There sat the Olvera House Superintendent Buchanan, Ben and Alison! He was so surprised that it was a chorus later before he realized what he was singing.

When they finished, Buchanan stood up and folding himself over the lectern, began: "J. Edgar Hoover says that our growing delinquency problem is the 'frontier of shame on the American scene.' And he knows. In recent years juvenile crime increased 70 per cent but the juvenile population only 16 per cent. In New York statistics, 41.2 per cent of arrests for all major crimes involve offenders under twenty-one. In Detroit, police estimate that 70 to 80 per cent of all thefts are committed by juveniles. Los Angeles and vicinity has the same problem, which we try to help solve by Olvera House activities."

Knox only half-listened as he stared at Alison's alert face and bright blue eyes. *She ought to be by my side.* Joan whispered, "Who's the girl?"

"Someone I used to know."

Buchanan sat down and Ben got up. "We have some great successes at Olvera House — boys who need only encouragement and Christian teaching to become respected citizens. But if I tell you of one of our failures, perhaps you'll understand better the imperative of the work. Christmas Eve a teen-age boy named Joe was missing from choir rehearsal. We were busy. It would have been too easy to go on without him, but I felt compelled to find out what had happened."

Knox remembered, *He and Alison were worried that night about some boy.*

"I went to his home, a two-room frame house in the poor district of Los Angeles. The mother was sobbing her heart out. Joe had been arrested as a narcotic addict! She knew the misery he faced trying to kick the habit in jail, the temptations he would face when released, never again to live a normal life. I have been permitted to visit him in the jail ward of the hospital, and to tell him of the forgiveness and strength in Christ."

As Ben talked his thin face glowed and Knox knew, *He's got something I haven't. Something that attracted Alison! What did she call it? Consecration!*

When Ben sat down, Buchanan got up again and his eyes swept the crowd as he said, "Olvera House regrets losing Ben and Alison, but they're getting married and going to Mexico, under the Biblical Translators. I don't know how many of you know of this organization but its members go to the Indian tribes in the interior of Mexico, reduce the tribal languages to writing, and translate the Bible into them.

"It is a faith mission. By that I mean that the members raise their own support; their relatives, friends and different churches pledge to send them a certain amount each month. In turn, they send out a monthly report of their work."

He went on to tell the amount of money Ben and Alison would need to go to Mexico. The ushers passed out cards for anyone interested in receiving the news letter to sign. Vince took one. Knox thought, *I ought to help, but it would hurt to hear about how happy she is with Ben. What have they got that I haven't? I've got to find out!*

After the benediction, Knox said, "I think I'll go to the Easter conference that the church is planning."

"I'll go along for the ride," Vince agreed.

"Did you say you were going to the retreat?" Joan asked.

"That's for sure!"

"Be our guest?" Vince invited.

"Sharon and I are going. Aren't we, Sharon?"

"It'll be a change."

The four of them made their way to the table where Frances Billings was taking reservations. Despite the chatter of the young people, Frances methodically took deposits, wrote down each person's name, assigned cabins, and gave directions to reach Mountain Top Camp.

"Isn't it wonderful that we're going together!" Joan said. Knox looked over Joan's shoulder at Alison, wondering if he ought to go speak to her. But she and Ben were busy talking to a young man. *I'd only be persona non grata.*

"I'll have a half-day off Good Friday from the cell block," Sharon said. "We can leave at a reasonable time."

"We'll pick you up," Knox promised.

Good Friday afternoon, he and Vince drove by the Vanden-Berg home in Pasadena and picked up Joan, Sharon and their luggage . . . two overnight cases, one suitcase, and a hat box. "You'd think you were going for a month!"

"We have to be beautiful for you boys," Sharon said.

Knox enjoyed driving, the feel of the wheel under his hands, the road spinning by. Joan sat close beside him, saying little. Sharon and Vince were in the back seat, laughing and chatting. They took the freeway to Ontario, and even after they left it, the road was smooth and fast, except for the last twenty miles up Mountain Top Road. It was graded, but the curves slowed Knox down.

Arriving at Mountain Top Camp, they left the car in the parking area and went to the office. There Frances Billings gave them mimeographed programs, meal tickets and keys to their cabins.

After seeing that the girls were settled, Knox and Vince went to their cabin. It was made of rough boards, furnished with six cots, stools and a board along the wall for a catch-all dressing table. They unpacked a few essentials. Then Knox stood in the center of the cabin, listening to the constant ripple of a near-by brook over its bed of stones.

Vince flopped on his cot. "Either these were designed as torture chambers, or to keep us out of them."

Knox studied his program. "I think the latter. They seem to have something going every minute."

Vince glanced at his. "Have to go to the meeting this evening, everyone will, but I can probably ditch the morning sessions, and, hurrah, there's recreation in the afternoon! Horseback riding, no less. I haven't been a half dozen times since I left Radio Island."

"Must be a beautiful spot!"

"It's the greatest! Just because I didn't get along with Dad, don't think I didn't have fun when I was a kid. I didn't spend my time sulking because the Great Redl was too busy to notice me. I went fishing, boating, and even had my own horse, Chief."

Knox stared at the block of time on Saturday's program, marked Recreation. That was one thing he didn't need. If at that time he could dodge his friends, he'd go by himself and do a little thinking.

With that as his secret goal, he enjoyed the meals, the meeting, the good humored companionship. The next day, after lunch, when the group enjoyed fun time, Vince gave his imitation of an Indian. It consisted of standing in one place wrapped in a blanket, grunting, while others tried to get him to talk. Vince's bland square face set everyone laughing.

Knox mumbled an excuse to Joan and slipped out of the dining room. On the porch he took a deep breath and his glance darted here and there. *Where shall I go? Not the cabin. Vince might follow me there. That brook that I hear murmuring all the time. Where is it? There must be some spot by it where I can be alone.*

He walked by the office, past the men's cabins, into a grove of trees. Between the tall redwoods the sun glittered on the carpet of fallen pine needles. The brook became more and more noisy until he stood on its bank and watched it ripple down the hill.

He flung himself on the rough ground, his body in the sun, his face in the shade of a tree. Gradually thoughts of the morning, of Vince's square face with a disturbed look, of Joan looking at him as if he were wonderful, faded, and he felt alone under the blue vault of sky, amidst the rustle of the trees, alone with God.

God! The Almighty had always been a part of his upbringing. Knox remembered that when he was small, Gramps used to set him upon his knee and sing the Psalms in meter to him. Gramp's example had counted, too. He was always spending the profits from his small grocery store to send a boy to camp or school. And when his wife died, MacLaren's face was taut with grief, but he quoted from Job, "The Lord gave and the Lord hath taken away; blessed be the name of the Lord."

And there was Lelia. He could see his mother's smiling face as she sat at her bedroom desk, studying her lesson for Sunday, or in the kitchen making Jello for the church luncheon, or baking peanut butter cookies for the children's hospital.

Then he thought of his father. Bull was a man's man if there ever was one. He wasn't one who talked of religion but he demanded fine-line honesty from himself, Knox, Stuart and the boys he trained. He went to church as regularly on Sunday as he went to gym on Monday. And when he lined up with the elders to serve communion he looked even more serious than when he urged his team to go out and win!

Church, too, had meant a lot to Knox. He remembered when he was nine and his teacher, Abbie Stewart, a too-thin, too-nervous woman, had urged him to "Let Jesus come into your heart." They had knelt together while he prayed. Then she had taken him to the minister and Knox stumbled over his words as he told the Reverend Aimes that he wanted to join the church. There had been a bubbling joy in his heart in those days.

Somehow he'd lost it. He still went to church, but mostly because of his training, not for the blissful joy of worship. Alison had been right. It had been his absorption in sports that had taken his mind away from God. He was a one-track sort of person. He had given his all to being champion and now he wanted to give his all to God, to serve Him!

He flung his arms back over his head, touching the bark of the tree, closed his eyes and prayed, "Lord, I'm going to live for You. I don't know what You want me to do. Maybe it is to be a coach as Dad is, maybe -----"

With a sudden feeling that it was not respectful to God to

pray lying on his back, he knelt. Taking a deep breath, he continued, "I don't know what You want me to do but I'm going to pray and read my Bible every day, and when I know what You want me to do, I'll do it and nothing will stop me. In Jesus' Name. Amen."

He waited, with a solemn hush in his heart, seeming to feel the approval of God. He knew, *Come what may, I belong to the Lord from the shoe laces of my trackshoes to my dreams!*

5

"O Woman, you are not merely the handiwork of
God, but also of men; these are ever endowing you
with beauty from their own hearts . . . You are one-
half woman and one-half dream."

Rabindranath Tagore

Knox rose, brushed the dust off his knees and stretched his
arms high over his head. *I feel good!* He walked to the stream,
watching it ripple by. It was more wide than deep and an uneven
path of stepping stones led to the quiet grove of trees on the other
side. *Perhaps I'll-----* Hearing the crunch of footsteps, he swung
around. "Joan!"

She came toward him, wearing a tan sheath skirt, copper belt
and pale green sweater. The bright sunlight caught the golden
sheen of her hair. "Why, Knox, I-----"

"You didn't go riding with the others?"

"I wanted to be alone, to think."

"So did I!"

She came to his side, smiled, then stared at the stream. "Let's
cross over."

He glanced at her small feet in trim flats and at the uneven
stepping stones. "I don't know if it would be safe for you."

"I think I can make it." With a low laugh, she stepped onto
the first stone, watching the water swirl about it. Then she stepped
onto the second stone. Knox stepped onto the first stone, covering
it completely with his feet.

Joan flung out her arms to balance herself and went from stone to stone, with Knox following her. Near the other side were two stones, farther apart than the others. She stepped onto the edge of the first one, then grabbed the air, trying to keep her balance. Knox jumped into the water and caught her, holding her steady. The water reached the calf of his leg and his face was even with hers. Her eyes shimmered. Hungrily his lips sought hers and he pulled her to him. Her slim body felt soft and warm against his. He drew his face away to catch his breath. She put her hand on his cheek, holding his face next to hers.

"Joan, you will marry me, won't you? You do love me, don't you?"

"More than anything in the world!"

He pressed his lips against hers, holding her close to him. The water babbled against the stones. She drew her mouth away, laughing, "You're standing in the water!"

"Who cares?"

"Silly, I care. You must get out of it." She brushed her lips against his, then walked across the two stones to the shore where she dropped on the dry ground. "Take off your shoes and dry your feet."

He sat beside her, his back against a rock, and took off his sneakers and socks. Joan laid the socks on a flat stone and set his shoes where the sun would shine in them. "There, they'll be dry soon."

"I don't care if they ever dry." He put his arm about her, drawing her close to him. "It beats winning all the medals in the world to have someone love you."

She put her head in the hollow of his shoulder. "You could get any girl at Mountain Top or Grace Church, or even UCLA."

He stared across the stream at the tree under which he had knelt a few minutes ago, and thought how losing a girl had driven him to God. "You remember that girl, Alison Franks, who came with Buchanan from Olvera House to Grace Church? The one with the beautiful eyes?"

"I remember her because you were so interested in her."

"I mention her only because I can't deceive you, Joan. It

wouldn't be fair. I used to go with Alison and just a few days before I met you, I asked her to marry me."

"And she wouldn't?"

"I wasn't good enough for her."

"How could she think such a thing!"

"But she was right, I wasn't sold out to God."

"But you're a Christian."

He sighed and repeated, "Christian — there are lots of different kinds in this world and I want to be the best. That's why I came out here to be alone, to give myself to God."

"How wonderful!"

"Joan, I want you to understand that though I love you dearly, I can offer you only third place in my life."

"Third place?" She looked troubled.

He enclosed her soft hand in his. "Perhaps if I explain you'll see what I mean. I must put God first, and then whatever work He would have me do. I'm not the kind of fellow who does things half-heartedly, but if you're willing for God and His service to come first, then we'll be married."

"I think you're wonderful! And we can be married in June. After you graduate, but before you begin coaching. That'll give us time for a honeymoon. I wouldn't graduate until next year, but I don't need to. A diploma doesn't mean everything to me. I'd rather be married. I know Mom will want us to be married at her church instead of Grace Church, but you won't mind that, will you? After all, the wedding is the bride's affair, isn't it?"

He nodded, feeling that he'd entered a track event about which he knew nothing, and the coach was telling him all the rules in one breath. Joan seemed tremendously full of plans for a girl who had only been proposed to a few minutes ago.

"I think I ought to have the princesses as my bridesmaids. They would expect to be. And I can have Sharon and Gloria as maids of honor. I'd like all the girls dressed in shades of pink. Would you like that?"

"Sure, Honey." He only half-listened, happy in the warmth of her love, until the shadows began to lengthen. Then he put on his shoes and they walked hand-in-hand back to camp.

He went to his cabin to wash up. Vince, stretched on the bed, asked, "Where have you been? We really had a ride! And will I know it tomorrow!"

"I'm the happiest man in the world."

"You look it! What's up?"

"Joan has promised to marry me."

"No!"

"What's wrong?"

"Nothing. I congratulate you. She's the greatest, but somehow I didn't expect you to go this far. After all, she caught you on the rebound," Vince half reminded, half accused.

"It's more than that," Knox defended, and partly to prove it, he decided, *I'll tell everyone,* making his plans.

After dinner the young people went up the hill to Victory Circle, an outdoor amphitheater on the hill behind the dining hall. Wooden benches were arranged in a semi-circle and at the center a small campfire glowed. Knox led Joan to the front row, with Vince and Sharon following. Vince whispered, "What's the idea of sitting on the mourner's bench?"

"I want to be handy, that's for sure."

Jones led the song service with his usual gusto, singing the hymns of the coming Easter, "Christ Arose" and "He Lives."

After the singing, Aunt Bea Aldrich, the young people's leader, put her large Bible on the lectern and wiped her palms on her green linen handkerchief. In a low pitched voice that carried to the highest tier of benches, she began to speak.

Knox was always absorbed by her talks. He fully understood why nearly five hundred college students came to her Sunday school class at Grace Church.

She was a tall, large-boned woman, with graying hair arranged in soft waves. She wore simple clothes, and neither jewelry nor makeup. But her face shone with an inner glow as she spoke on the meaning of Easter, concluding, "Tomorrow is the glad Easter Day of Christendom. It will be celebrated around the world, by pilgrimages to the holy city of Jerusalem, by secret believers in Russia, by aborigines in New Zealand. The most heart-warming way to celebrate it is by giving our lives to the One who gave His life for us. Here -----" she waved her hand toward a small pile of wood, "are fagots. Let us hum, 'Take my life and let is be, consecrated Lord to Thee,' and I hope each one of you will put a fagot on the fire, telling of your decision to follow Christ."

The stars overhead, the tall pine trees, the surrounding darkness increased Knox's feeling of solemnness. *This is my chance.*

He squeezed Joan's hand, jumped up and stepped to the small kindling-wood fire. He picked up a fagot and stared at the tier after tier of white patches that he knew were faces. "When I won the Olympic decathlon championship I thought that was the thrill of a lifetime. I'll never forget the cheering crowd, but today I had an even greater thrill. I gave everything I have, from the laces of my track shoes to my dreams, to God. I don't know yet what He wants me to do, but whatever it is, I'll do it. A little later the most beautiful girl in the world promised to marry me, willing to take third place in my life."

Knox could see Vince's face in the light of the fire. His jaw had fallen open as if he were shocked by Knox's announcement. The young people began whispering. He realized that he would have to explain more fully. "I mean that God comes first, then His service second, and my wife third. With that agreement, Joan VandenBerg promised to marry me. Didn't you, Joan?"

He beckoned to her. With uncertain steps she walked toward him. He gave her hand a reassuring squeeze. She picked up a fagot and waited beside him.

"May the burning of this fagot be a symbol of the way I want my life to burn out for God!" He threw the fagot into the center of the fire, where it caught fire and blazed brightly.

"And I -----" Joan faltered and threw her fagot toward the fire. It fell a little short of the blaze. Knox kicked it into the fire.

Joan ran to her seat and buried her face in her hands. Sharon patted her. Knox sat down, edged Sharon away and put his arm protectingly around Joan.

Aunt Bea stepped near the flickering fire, a strained look on her face. "The example of these two young people giving their

lives to God is heart-warming. Are there others who want to
follow Christ?"

Knox sat there, warmed by an inner feeling of serenity,
watching others go forward and put their fagots on the fire. He
wondered if Vince would, but he only sat beside Knox, looking
bored. Knox realized that though Vince went willingly to Grace
Church, Vince had never had the feeling of abandonment to God
that he had experienced that afternoon.

The young people began singing and then slowly drifted down
the hill. Vince and Sharon started down the path. Knox, carefully holding Joan's arm, started after them. Aunt Bea came up to
Knox. "I want to talk to you."

He nodded, hesitating.

"Go on, Joan. Knox and I will join you."

"But -----" Joan objected.

"Go on. I want to speak to Knox, alone."

"I'll wait at the foot of the path," Joan said as, with a smile
that said "hurry," she went down the path between the tall trees.

"I want to speak to you about asking Joan to be third in your
life. You're too consecrated for her. She doesn't understand what
she's promised."

"But she does. I'm sure she does." *I've offered Joan what
Alison wanted.*

"Joan's a warm-hearted girl, but also she wants what most
girls want in life, a home, children, financial security, things no
man sold out to God can give a girl. I don't think even you
understand what sort of life you're asking Joan to share."

"But I'm sure." He started after Joan, and, catching a
glimpse of her golden hair shining under one of the path lights,
quickened his step.

6

"To him who gives is given corn, water, wine, the world, the starry heaven."

Masefield

Picking out Joan's engagement ring had been a heart-warming experience, but as Knox drove back to the frat house, he realized that the rings and his wedding expenses would clean out his savings. Between college and the Olympics, he hadn't been able to work much. Bull gave him an allowance and he had a part-time job for USCLA News Bureau that enabled him to keep his amateur standing.

He parked in his usual place, then walked up to his room, trying to figure out some way to make some extra money. Vince was lying on the bed reading, with the radio turned on. Knox recognized the warm, vibrant voice of Vince's dad, saying, "I wish you could see the tremendous beauty and the terrific need on Radio Island. It abounds in beauty, the tall pine trees almost to the shore, the ------"

Vince asked, "How was the prize date?"

Knox leaned against the dresser, facing Vince. "We picked out the rings. I'm going to cut classes tomorrow, go to Santa Ana and get the money out of the bank."

"You'll find that rose queens don't come cheap!"

"I didn't expect her to. I especially want her to have an engagement ring. It settles things for me and others."

"What gives?"

"Remember the Christmas Eve when I went to see Alison?"

41

"How could I forget? No one wants to see his best friend turned down."

"She was already engaged to Ben Moore but she wasn't wearing a ring and so, like a fool, I went ahead and proposed. If she'd been wearing a ring, maybe I could have saved myself the embarrassment of running a race someone else had already won."

"Couldn't this Moore scrape together the price of even one-hundredth of a carat?"

"It wasn't that. Instead, as a present for her, he sent the money to the American Bible Society."

"He what?" Vince exclaimed.

Knox nodded and the two friends stared at each other as Hymie Redl's voice continued, "My friends, this is a tremendous opportunity for you to be a blessing to others. These Indian young men and girls have come to us begging to know more of God. And we have welcomed them, holding Bible classes for them. At first they were held in open air. But can you imagine the distractions of meeting out-of-doors? Every eye turns when a bird wings by, or a motor boat chugs up to the wharf. So by faith we built an auditorium, not an expensive one, but plain wooden boards and crude benches, a shelter from the wind and rain. We chopped our own trees and planed our own boards. Radio Island people are not afraid of work. But it still cost over one thousand dollars and we need your help.

"Wouldn't it be tremendous if someone sent us enough for the entire building? We would, with grateful hearts, name the hall after that person. But we dare not expect that much. Instead, we ask that each one of you ask God what He would have you do. Send one hundred or one dollar, whatever you can afford. You will be a blessing if you do. Will you write us? Tonight? I'll look forward to hearing from you."

Vince swung around on the bed, turned off the radio and squinted his small eyes, "When you told the gang at Mountain Top of your engagement to Joan, you said you were both going to put God first. Why don't you do what this fellow Moore did? Send the engagement ring money to Dad and give the receipt to Joan?"

"That is something! But I'd need the receipt for Sunday, when her mother's having a family gathering to announce our engagement."

"Air mail the money tomorrow to Lyle — that's the bookkeeper — and ask him to air mail the receipt."

Knox tried to estimate the good his money would do on Radio Island, invested in an auditorium where the Indians would hear the message of God for years. *Surely Joan would value that above any diamond ring!* "Thanks for the suggestion."

The next day after his eleven o'clock class, he drove to Santa Ana and drew the necessary money out of the bank. He went to the jeweler's and bought a cheaper set of rings, then made out a money order for one hundred dollars to Hymie Redl, asking him to air mail the receipt. And he would give some money to Ben and Alison as he had felt he should. He phoned Olvera House, making an appointment to see Ben early Sunday afternoon.

The rest of the week was taken by classes and study. Twice he folded himself into the small telephone booth on the first floor of the frat house and talked to Joan. He didn't tell her his surprise, wanting to see her joy when he gave her the two receipts.

Saturday Redl's receipt arrived air mail, special, as Vince had said it would. And Sunday, after church, he headed for Olvera House.

It was easy to park near Olvera House, as that district of Los Angeles was deserted on Sunday. He went down the hall, to the door of Alison's craft room. He could hear the chatter of children's voices and Alison's smooth voice giving instructions, "You make the head out of a damp wad of newspaper."

He stepped inside the craft room. Alison, in a blue smock, was seated on a child's chair, shaping a puppet's head out of newspaper. Three junior-age Mexican girls were watching her. She looked up. "Hello, Knox, it's good to see you. Ben will be here soon, I hope. He went after some boys who want to make puppets."

"I see," he said and realized why he had once loved her. She was pretty with her wide blue eyes and her smoky hair, but also she had an air of assurance. A man could depend on her!

"Meet Dolores, Anita and Consuelo. Girls, this is Knox Taylor, Olympic decathlon champion."

Knox smiled at the girls. They were about twelve and all dressed in Sunday white. Anita and Consuelo squealed with delight, but Dolores drew back bashfully, trying to hide behind Alison.

"You'd better clear off a corner of the table and sit down. I really can't promise when Ben will be here. If he has a fault, it's being late."

"I see." He leaned against the cluttered craft table.

"Even that really isn't his fault. He tries to do too much and lets people take up his time."

"I hope he won't be too late. I'm due at Joan's house in half an hour. But perhaps you haven't heard. She and I are engaged."

"Oh, are you? That's perfect!" A look of relief crossed her face.

"And don't let me disturb you. Go on with your work."

"I'm afraid I must, but you can tell me about Joan as I work." She got up and placed the soggy head on the table to dry. Then she pulled a piece of white cloth toward her and said to the girls, "We will draw the puppet's face."

Knox watched her, realizing that though Alison was relieved that he had found someone else, she wasn't too interested in hearing about the girl he loved. *Could she be a little jealous?*

She picked up a thick black crayon and drew eyebrows for the face. Anita leaned over, getting between Alison and the drawing. Alison pushed her gently aside and began drawing the eyes. As she worked deftly, yet kept the girls in line, he realized, *I'm glad Joan doesn't have Alison's efficiency. It makes her need me more.*

Alison finished the face and began cutting out the puppet's clothes. The girls watched and asked questions. She answered them in her even tone of voice. Knox grew impatient. Ben didn't come, and time was going by. Mrs. VandenBerg wouldn't like it if he were late! He glanced at his watch. "Alison, I can't wait any longer. I'll be late."

She put down her scissors and nodded to the girls to be quiet. "I'm sorry. I don't know what has delayed him. Perhaps I can give him a message."

"Maybe that is best!" He drew out of his pocket an envelope with ten ten-dollar bills in it and explained, "I was so impressed by Ben's giving you an American Bible Society receipt for your engagement present that I wanted to do as much for Joan. I sent part of our money to Hymie Redl, the Canadian radio pastor."

"Vince's father?"

"Yes, and I want to give some of it to you and Ben for your outfit for Mexico."

"How dear of you! Ben is so generous, he needs things for himself. I wonder, Knox, would you let me use the money to buy Ben a watch? Maybe if he had a watch he wouldn't always be late. And he'll never take the money to buy one for himself."

"Sure, and I must hurry." *Anything to make her happy!*

She took the money and put it in her smock pocket. "Ben will thank you. Good-by."

"It was good seeing you again." He strode to the door. There he paused and looked back. Alison, her eyes alive with interest, was explaining more about the puppet making to the girls. A half tinge of regret stirred in his heart and he reminded himself, *But I love Joan.*

7

"Woman is the salvation or the destruction of the family. She carries its destiny in the folds of her mantle."

Amiel

As Knox walked up the path of the VandenBerg house, he could hear the sound of voices and knew, *I won't be able to see Joan alone as I should.* He rang the bell. Joan, her face flushed, came to the door. "Knox, you're late! Mom has been wondering where you were."

He stepped into the large living room. It had always struck him as overdone with its thick saffron rug, and overstuffed furniture upholstered in yellow and crimson chrysanthemums on an ivory background.

"We were worried, positively worried," said Florence Vanden-Berg, as she came toward Knox. "I just knew you couldn't be purposely late on a day like today, of all days."

"I'm sorry. I was waiting for a man, but he didn't show up, so I left." *Does she always make others feel as if they are wrong?*

Florence VandenBerg was a blonde in her middle forties. And while she carried more weight than her daughter, she dressed as if she were one of the girls, wearing a green dress with white Egyptian chariots running all over it, and triple strands of crystals. "It's only right that you did! We've been waiting."

Pete VandenBerg walked up to Knox, and with a welcoming look in his blue eyes, gave him a firm handclasp. Knox had seen Pete only when surrounded by his bevy of bright, talkative women, but he felt he would like the short, stocky man if he had the opportunity to know him.

"Hi, Handsome," Sharon called. Knox turned and automatically smiled at her. She always looked like a doll just taken out of a box. And this afternoon she wore a violet dress with a tight bodice and full skirt that accentuated each curve.

Joan put her hand a little tighter on Knox's arm, and led him to the divan. "This is my sister, Gloria."

Gloria, the oldest of the three VandenBerg girls, was another blonde, with a polished air, attractively dressed in pink plaid. Beside her was a fair-haired miniature of three.

"It's about time we met," Gloria said.

"That's for sure."

"And this is my Susan Marie."

Susan Marie, in her matching pink plaid dress, stared at Knox with big blue eyes and drew closer to her mother.

"And this is Harvey Walker, Gloria's husband," Joan led Knox to a young man standing by the fireplace.

"Welcome to the ranks of brave men who marry VandenBerg women." Harvey shook Knox's hand.

"Harvey, don't tease! Knox won't understand," Joan said.

"He will, in time. Too well!"

Harvey is joking only in the sense that often if one speaks the truth, it is funny because it is unexpected.

"I hear you're decathlon champion. Tell me about the big event," Harvey continued.

Knox told him of his European experiences and sized up Harvey . . . six or seven years older than he, thick, black wavy hair, a well-developed body beginning to acquire padding. Knox asked, "Were you in the army?"

"I put in eighteen months overseas. How did you happen to dodge our peacetime army with the sergeants giving maid service?"

"So far, college deferments. But my brother, Stuart plans to join the air force."

"Boys, no secrets," Florence called. "Come, tell me just everything."

Knox sat on the divan between Joan and her mother. On the

other divan, along the wall, Harvey joined his wife and daughter. Sharon sat on a straight chair with her legs crossed and her arms hanging down at her sides, consciously forming a picture. On the edge of the group in an easy chair sat Pete, as if he were not a part of these chatting women. Knox even wondered if his hearing aid were turned on.

"Do tell me just everything!" Florence repeated.

"I suppose Joan told you that I accepted a job on the athletic staff at UCLA."

"You don't say! That ought to be interesting!" Harvey said.

"I'm trained for that kind of work but also I do some speaking at boys' clubs and I'm not sure but what I want to devote more of my time to boys."

"As a hobby, you mean?" Florence gave him a patronizing smile.

"Boys could never be a hobby to me. Gramps was always bringing home a stray boy to help and Dad has coached several crack football players."

"This is all too serious for me." Florence stood up. "Come, Sharon help me."

"You, too," Sharon glanced at Gloria and the sisters followed their mother into the kitchen.

"Florence has learned the secret of eating her cake and having it too," Harvey chuckled, as her substantial form disappeared through the kitchen door.

"I wish you wouldn't tease Mom," Joan defended and followed her sisters.

"How'd you happen to train for the Olympics?" Harvey asked Knox.

"That's easy! I figured there were thirty-three All-Americans each year but only one Olympic decathlon champion every four years, so being the lone wolf type, I accepted the decathlon challenge."

"Training takes your time, doesn't it?" Pete asked, moving onto the edge of his chair.

"Sure does! Even if you take a girl out and you pass a field,

you stop and throw your shotput a few times so the evening won't
be a total loss."

Pete and Harvey laughed and the men discussed Knox's training until Florence returned, wheeling a service cart. Sharon came
behind her carrying a silver cake cutter, Gloria carried the silver
percolator and Joan the pink napkins.

Florence pushed the service cart in front of Knox. On it was
a heart-shaped cake frosted with pink roses and twined hearts, on
a tall milkwhite cake stand, set in a centerpiece of white gardenias.

"Just a little something to welcome you into the family,"
Florence said. "Joanie, you cut the cake."

Sharon passed her sister the cake slicer. Joan cut the cake
and Florence poured the coffee. When everyone was served,
Florence sat beside Knox. He ate his cake, thinking, *The frosting
is too rich, and so is the cake.*

Florence put her empty cup and dish on the cart and looked
directly at Knox. "Do show us the ring! Joanie said you were
bringing it today. And don't mind our being here when you give
it to her. We always do everything, positively everything as a
family. Besides, she's seen it already."

But I must talk to her first!

"It's all right, Knox."

Knox pressed his lips together, reached into his pocket and
took out the box and the envelope with the receipt. Then he
hesitated. The family smiled encouragingly at him. Knox gulped,
"I hope you all realize how thankful I am to have a dear girl like
Joan promise to be my wife. When we became engaged, we
agreed that we wanted to give God first place in our lives. And,
while I've not been able to discuss this with Joan, I'm sure she'll
be pleased with what I've done."

The smile faded from Joan's face. Florence, Gloria and
Sharon gave him identical stares. Pete fussed with the knob of
his hearing aid, while Harvey gave Knox a questioning glance.
Little Susan Marie slowly nibbled her cake.

"When Joan and I looked at rings, she selected a set costing
over four hundred dollars. I would have gladly given it to her
because nothing is too good for Joan, but on thinking the matter

over, I decided I could give Joan something better than a ring, and that was a share in the Kingdom of God. I sent part of the money to Hymie Redl's radio program and bought a cheaper set."

"You did what?" Florence gasped.

"I sent one hundred dollars to the Bright Day Broadcasting Association and bought a smaller set for Joan." He pressed the front of the box and the lid flipped open.

Florence grasped the box and stared at the ring. "How could you do such a thing to my Joanie? Don't you realize that she has to show this ring to all her friends so they can see what kind of man she's marrying?"

Sharon stared over her mother's shoulder at the small diamond. "And now let one and all understand why I don't get married. The male ego is too busy doing hand springs for the applause of others to give any girl first place in his life."

Knox's face drained white at the mangling of his motives.

"There are other things besides rings," Gloria said. Susan Marie stopped eating and stared at her scowling grandmother. Gloria drew the child closer to her. Harvey smiled as if to say, *Now you understand!*

"You must get your money back!"

"But I can't."

"What do you mean you can't? You can do what is right for Joanie."

Pete stood quietly to his feet and in a low voice, said, "Flo, I wouldn't say that."

Joan took the ring from her. "You don't understand Knox. He means all right."

Knox relaxed at Joan's defense. "Please, let me explain."

"You have nothing to explain! Your actions speak louder than words," Florence answered, staring defiantly at her husband.

Tears filled Joan's eyes and she hurried out of the room, across the lanai. Knox followed her across the tiled patio, between the rows of rose bushes and camellias, until she came to a bench. There she sat down sobbing. He put his arm around her and held her until she stopped trembling.

"How could you do this awful thing to me? How could you?"

"But you said to your mother ------"

"I defended you to Mom, but it's awful. You had no right to throw the money away."

"But, Honey, I didn't throw it away, I ------" He passed her the crumpled envelope.

She stared at the receipt, frowning, "But this didn't take all that was left."

If she knew I gave one hundred dollars to Alison to buy a watch, she really would be upset. He avoided answering by saying, "Honey, I thought you'd be pleased."

She took the handkerchief out of his coat pocket and wiped her eyes. "I'm just shocked. I wanted Mom to like you. It will have to be all right, only . . . ."

"Yes, Honey?"

"You must let Mom have her way about the wedding. She wasn't happy about Gloria and Harvey when they eloped. Mom has always wanted her daughters to have big church weddings."

"Anything to please you, Honey." He took the ring from her and, taking her left hand, slipped the ring on the proper finger. She held it up, letting it flicker in the sunlight. "It's not too awful and later you can change it for a bigger one."

"Yes, Honey." He pulled her close to him.

She nestled her head on his shoulder and sighed. "You've got to learn to get along with Mom. She means well. Her whole life is us girls."

"I'll apologize. Anything."

Harvey walking toward them, called, "Florence has cooled down. Pete's talking to her and she'd like you to come back."

"Oh, we must!" Joan jumped up and hurried toward the house.

Knox started after her with Harvey falling in step beside him. Harvey laughed. "These VandenBerg women! You get beauty when you get one, but they cost plenty."

8

"Someone says 'Boys will be boys': he forgot to add, 'Boys will be men.' "

Unknown

Pete had convinced Florence that she could explain to her friends that Joanie and her fiancé were "too, too" self-sacrificing. So she forgave Knox, treating him as if he were an irresponsible boy who mustn't err again. And Gloria and Harvey invited him out to dinner, "Where," Harvey said, "I can brief you on the care and feeding of VandenBerg women."

With a feeling of frustration that Knox couldn't define, the days slipped into May . . . a mixture of term papers, examinations, wedding invitations and caterers' menus. The families met properly, and after that, meetings and phone calls were frequent, discussing each detail of the wedding.

Along with the demands of his coming graduation and wedding Knox was speaking at boys' clubs and men's dinners. Aunt Bea had made the arrangements and the listeners thrilled to hear a prize athlete tell of his belief in Christ. But the thought nagged Knox, *I'm talking too much about boys and doing too little for them.*

One Friday, early in June, Aunt Bea arranged for him to speak in Ventura at the closing meeting of a boys' basketball league. The trip took all afternoon. Afterwards, he stopped for dinner at a roadside café and then headed south through San Fernando Valley.

When he reached North Valley City, he remembered, *This*

*is where Gloria and Harvey live. I think I'll drop by and see
them. And little Susan Marie.* He had brought Joan out one
Sunday for dinner, so he was sure he could find the place at the
end of Bougainvillea Drive.

When he reached the house there were no lights in the
windows, but he parked, thinking, *Gloria and Harvey may be in
the back.* He crossed the wide lawn and walked down the driveway, alongside the house to the patio. He paused. There was a
light in the kitchen, and blaring from the radio was "Red Alli-
gators." Knox shook his head. *That's not Gloria's kind of music.*

He strode to the door, lifted his hand to knock and stiffened.
Through the window he saw a teen-age boy. *Who's that?* The boy
was about sixteen, wearing blue jeans and T-shirt, with a mop of
uncombed brown hair. *I'm sure this is the right house, but that
boy? He's painting something.* Knox gasped - - - - *He's painting
Gloria's pink cupboards with streaks of red!*

He edged closer to the window and stared. The boy was
playing tick-tack-toe with red paint on the pink wall. Winning the
game with X's, he put the brush in the paint can and walked
across the room to the stove. Knox stretched to watch him. The
boy opened the oven door, took out a cake and carried it out of
sight.

*He's gone to the snack bar to eat. I've got to get him. If I
go in the door, he will run through the dining room and out a
window.* He glanced around and, seeing a metal patio chair, eased
it under the doorknob to block the door. Then he went to the
side of the house and, finding a bedroom window open, climbed
in. *I guess this is how the boy got in!*

Stealthily he crossed the darkened living room to the dining
room. The rhythm of "Whoo-oo-oo, Baby! I'm having me some
fun tonight, yeah," shrilled from the kitchen radio. Knox eased
the swinging door a crack and saw the boy seated at the snack
bar eating a hunk of cake and drinking a bottle of coke. Knox
pushed open the door. "Hello."

The boy jumped up, dashed for the back door and tugged at
it. Knox sprang behind him and pinned his arms to his sides,

holding him as easily as he would a wobbly vaulting pole. "All I want is to talk to you."

"Go ahead, you louse, and turn me in to the cops! See if I care! I got plenty of record and I might as well have a little more. They can't do nothing to me, I'm a minor."

"You can sure wreck a place!" Knox stared at the kitchen. The linoleum had been cut in strips and was rolled up. The walls were covered with big and little tick-tack-toe squares. A ham had been taken out of the refrigerator and hacked at. Two soiled mixing bowls were on the drainboard. "Why did you do it?"

"I don't know."

"But you must."

"I don't know. A guy's gotta do something for fun, ain't he?"

"But not this! Come, talk to me." Knox relaxed his hold.

The boy wiggled free and faced him. "You're strong, ain't you? Who are you? A wrestler or something?"

"Track's my line. My name is Knox Taylor."

The boy's eyes bugged out. "I know you. You're the guy what won the Olympic decathlon championship. I saw you on TV. It must be swell to be a champ. Was it a ton of work? Did you know for sure you'd win?"

"It was a lot of work, and I was far from being sure I'd win." Knox clicked off the radio, then, taking the boy by the shoulder, led him to the snack bar. They sat down and, after the boy cut Knox a piece of cake, he listened while Knox explained, "Dad helped me to take one-fifth of a minute off my high hurdle by having me knock three nickels off the hurdle without knocking it over. I'd been jumping too high."

"That's the most!"

"And how about you? What's your name?"

The boy slumped on his stool, a sullen expression on his face. "Leon Nye."

"Where do you live?"

"In a housing project down the street."

"With your parents?"

"Kinda."

"What do you mean, 'kinda'?"

"Mom and the Old Man live in the house and I live in a lean-to at the back."

"You're the only child?"

"Nope, there's Roxie. But she's married."

"What made you come here tonight?"

Leon glaced around the kitchen. "Maybe it is a mess, but I didn't start out to muck it up, only to see the joint. My mom works where Mr. Walker does. When Mom said she heard the Walkers was going to visit their in-laws tonight, I decided I wanted to see what a swell joint looked like. I climbed in the window and looked around. It ain't as swell as I thought it'd be."

"Go on," Knox encouraged. He was touched by the casual telling of the story by this underprivileged boy.

"When I spotted the linoleum, I kinda figured I'd like it on my floor and I knew Mr. Walker could get some more. I looked around until I found a sharp knife, then I took it up."

"You sure did!"

"I figured they wouldn't be home for a while and I was hungry, so I found some ham and made a couple of sandwiches. Then I decided I wanted some cake, so I found some cake mix and baked it. And while I was waiting, I found some red paint and thought I'd fix up the kitchen for Mrs. Walker."

"Now I've caught you, what are you going to do about it?"

"The Old Man will beat me and Mom will pay for what's wrecked. They always do."

That isn't any answer. "Do you ever go to Sunday school?"

"Once or twice when I was a little kid. But I'm too old."

"Do your folks go?"

"Nope. They like to sleep late Sunday."

"I go."

"You, a champ?"

"Sure, every Sunday. How'd you like to be friends with me?"

"Would you teach me to sprint? I'm a good size for a sprinter."

Knox nodded. The boy was a runt, short and thin because of lack of proper nourishment; not because he had the compact body of a runner. "Sure, only you'll have to clean up this mess."

"Whatchamean?"

"Come out tomorrow with me and we'll paint this kitchen pink again. Your mom can buy the paint and new linoleum and we'll lay it."

"Sounds kinda dumb!"

"It's the right thing to do, Leon. If you bust something up, you ought to fix it, shouldn't you?"

Leon hung his head and mumbled, "I guess so."

"And to start, we'll wash the dishes now."

"You gonna help me?" Leon stared, wide-eyed at Knox.

"Sure."

"I never thought I'd see no champ washing dishes. My Old Man wouldn't wash no dishes if he had to eat on dirty ones. He says washing dishes is for dames and sissies."

"I don't see it that way. If I eat on the dishes, I can wash them."

"You're the most!" Leon said, and even though he did it half-grudgingly, he helped Knox clean the kitchen.

Knox put the last dish on the shelf and thought happily. *This is something! Bringing out the potential of a boy like Leon! I'd rather be doing it than teaching boys to run.* Anxious to report both the damage and progress, he said, "Come on, I'm going to phone Mrs. Walker."

"She'll have a fit! I know dames. They ain't for peace, never."

"She'll listen to what I say."

"I guess being champ counts, even with dames."

They went into the living room, where Knox sat in an easy chair and Leon on the footstool beside him. Knox picked up the phone. *I'm going to make Mrs. VandenBerg angry again. She'll think I ought to turn Leon over to the police. But all they'd do would be to lock him up.* He dialed the VandenBerg number.

Leon cocked his head and listened while Knox talked to Harvey, explaining the situation, "As long as the boy makes things right, don't you think that's more important than turning him over to the police?"

"Never saw where jail cured anyone, but a little hard work

might slow the boy down," Harvey agreed. "And now excuse me
if I hang up. Gloria and Mrs. V. are having a double fit trying
to find out what's happened."

"Tell Gloria that Leon and I will be here in the morning for
sure." He hung up the receiver. "I'm backing you, Leon, because I think you've got the stuff in you to be a winner."

"It don't sound like no picnic, but I won't let you down."

"Good boy! And now let's see your parents and explain
what's happened."

"Mom will yak like everything."

"Leon ----" Knox began, thinking Leon should show more
respect to his parents, but he decided, *Maybe I'd better meet
Leon's parents before I boost them.*

Knox and Leon went out to Knox's car and he drove three
blocks to a sea of quonset hut houses. Here and there someone
had planted a few geraniums or bought a slightly different number
plate. Otherwise, each house was identical.

Leon opened his door and went inside. Knox stepped in
behind him. The small room was dark except for a light over the
TV set. In an armchair, with her feet on an Ottoman, was a slight
woman dressed in a red blouse and dark blue slacks, eating pop
corn. She didn't look up, but kept watching the TV western.

"Mom, we got company."

"Friend of yours?"

"Yeah."

"Then tell him to wait until the commercial."

Leon waved Knox to sit down on the divan. Knox watched
the moving figures until the announcer began plugging the delights
of a western beer.

Mrs. Nye took a cigarette out of a pack, tapped it, lit it, and
turned to Leon, "What's on your mind?"

"Mom, I got a swell guy with me. Knox, this is my mom,
Willie Lou."

"Pleased to meet you."

"Mom, he's Knox Taylor, the decathlon champion."

"It's always swell, being any kind of a champ."

She doesn't even know what decathlon means!

"You boys entertain yourselves. A western's coming on."

"Mom, listen, won't you? Mr. Taylor's got something to tell you about me."

"You've been in mischief again? If you have, I'll have your dad beat you within an inch of your life. I don't know what I ever did to deserve having a boy like you. What's he done, mister?"

Trying to talk louder than the TV, Knox told how he had discovered Leon and the mess in the Walkers' home.

"A boy's got to have some fun. I've got to expect that. But I wish I was back in Wrangle on the ranch. There, you never had to watch a kid. He had miles to play in and nothing he could hurt."

"Mom, listen, will you? The champ's going to help me paint the kitchen tomorrow if you'll buy the paint and linoleum."

"I ought not to do it. I ought to make you get out and earn the money yourself, but you'd never do it, you lazy, good-for-nothing. What'll it cost?"

Knox took a deep breath. *The woman has no comprehension of right or wrong. Just her own comfort! How can Leon be expected to know anything!* He tried to estimate what the damage would cost to repair. He and Mrs. Nye had come to an agreement on price when the door opened. A man, broad of shoulders and paunchy, dressed in work clothes, stepped in.

"Al, Leon's been at it again, mucking up stuff. This time the man says we got to pay for it. And plenty, too!"

"Why, you little mutt!" Nye struck Leon across the face, knocking him to the floor in front of the TV, jarring it.

"Look out, Al, you'll hurt the set!" Willie Lou half-screamed.

Al kicked Leon as he lay on the floor. Leon whimpered and crawled away. "What's the mutt done?"

Heartsick, Knox told how Leon had messed up the Walker house, but that he and Leon were going to repair the damage.

"I guess it's all that we can do now you caught him, but folks ought to keep their doors locked so punk kids can't get in."

"You come by in the morning, I'll give you the dough," Willie Lou chimed in.

"We got it, with both of us working," Nye bragged. "It's

only if we got money to spend, Willie Lou and me likes to spend it on ourselves."

Knox agreed to come back in the morning and said goodby. He stepped outside and then stiffened as he heard the snap of a belt whirling through the air, followed by Leon's scream of pain. He put his hand back on the knob but checked himself, *I couldn't reason with Nye. He's punishing Leon as he thinks right. But it won't do any good. What Leon needs is kindness and the Lord.*

He got into his car and drove toward the frat house, full of the coming day's plans. Suddenly he remembered, *I'm supposed to discuss church decorations with Joan. I can't do it. She'll have to understand. And explain to Florence!*

9

"The maximum achievement of any man's life, after it is all over, is to have done the will of God. No man or woman can do more with a life."

Henry Drummond

I'll phone Joan from her sister's, Knox decided as he drove toward the Valley the next morning. When he reached the Nyes' he saw that Leon had a black eye, but said nothing in front of Mrs. Nye. She fussed at the "dumb expenses" but counted out the money. Only when he and Leon were in his car did Knox ask, "Where did you get the shiner?"

"The Old Man gave it to me for getting into this mess. He says he'll close 'em for keeps if I cost him dough again."

"I see." But, sick at heart, he thought, *Fists only make a boy sneaky.*

They picked up Gloria and drove to the store. There he paced the aisle while Gloria picked out the paint and the linoleum. *She's as fussy as her mother when it comes to shade.* She took so long that Knox knew he wouldn't have time to lay the linoleum. Out of his own wallet he paid the man to do it.

Even so, it was past time for his date with Joan when they reached the Walkers'. There, with Gloria, Leon, Harvey and Susan Marie watching, he called the VandenBerg number.

"Knox!" Joan exclaimed. "Where are you? Mom has lunch ready and we're waiting for you."

"I'm at Gloria's." He glanced at his audience. *Everything has to be a family affair with Joan.*

"At Gloria's! Of all places! At this time of day?"

"You know what happened last night and I'm here, trying to help Leon right things."

"But Knox, the woman from the florist is here to plan the decoration."

"I'll be there as soon as I can, but surely helping straighten out a boy is more important than a few flowers."

There was the sound of sobbing over the phone.

"Honey, don't cry! I have to help Leon. Don't you see?"

Harvey gave him a wise smile and walked into the kitchen.

"Give me the phone," Gloria said, "and I'll explain to her. After all, it's my kitchen that was wrecked. You go eat your lunch and get to work."

"Thanks." He watched for a minute as Gloria talked to Joan. Apparently she wasn't convincing her sister easily and so taking Leon with him, he went into the kitchen. Harvey helped them fix sandwiches.

"You got your troubles, Champ," Leon said. "That's dames for you. They don't help a fellow. Never."

"It's just that the wedding is important to a girl."

"Yes, it's their show!"

Knox had finished eating his lunch by the time Gloria came into the kitchen. "Don't worry, Knox. Mom thinks you don't pay enough attention to her queen daughter and so she upsets Joan, but she's a sweet girl. I told her Harvey'd go after her so she can help, too."

"Why didn't I think of that?"

"Mostly because you're not used to thinking in terms of we, us and our. Now, get along, Harvey."

"Always obey orders, Knox, it's quicker than arguing," Harvey said lightly as he went out the back door.

"Let's get to work!" Knox said. It took them about an hour to apply a white coat, then they had to wait two hours before they could apply the pink paint. They went outdoors and stretched out on the patio chairs. The sun was high and it was pleasant to relax.

"It takes longer to fix up stuff than it does to muck it up," Leon admitted plaintively.

"I've an idea that is one of the great truths of the ages. Did your parents teach you that?"

"They never taught me and Roxie nothin'. They never had no time for us. When we was home they always sent us off to movies, or left us alone while they went dancin'."

"But they must have taught you something."

"Sure, to lie about my age so I could get into the movies at half price. And then have a fit if I swiped the price of a movie out of Mom's purse. I don't figure her out."

"Your mom means well but she doesn't think things through," Knox answered carefully. *I mustn't destroy what meager respect Leon does have for his parents.*

"I think maybe Roxie and me was just in Mom's and the Old Man's way."

There was the sound of a car stopping in the driveway and in a few seconds Joan and Harvey came toward them. Knox jumped to his feet, thinking he had never seen her look lovelier. Her vivid pink sweater gave color to her fair skin and her hair looked like spun gold. Knox introduced Leon to her.

"Ain't I getting in with swell folks!"

They sat down again and Knox began telling her of their project. Joan sympathized with Gloria over her wrecked kitchen. Knox enjoyed having Joan with them. It was as if the arms of his heart held her when he looked at her. *It means everything to have a girl like Joan love me!*

"Are we here to talk or paint?" Leon broke into his thoughts.

Knox jumped up, "Come on, Harvey, how about you helping?" *Being with Joan made me forget Leon. I mustn't do that.*

"I could help paint my own kitchen," Harvey said, and the three men went into the house, going to work.

It was late when they finished and Knox took Leon and Joan home. Life became a flurry of graduation week . . . last-minute grades . . . special church service honoring the grads . . . farewell luncheon at the frat house . . . special dinner honoring the head coach and the baccalaureate. People kept congratulating Knox on becoming a member of UCLA's staff while Knox kept thinking of Leon.

One evening, when he and Vince were alone, he told him about Leon. "He needs a friend, someone who'll help him."

"Like you did me!"

Knox stared at Vince in surprise and then remembered how their friendship had begun. Sometime in their freshman year, on the track, he began to notice Vince. He was a flip sort of fellow and didn't make friends, too inclined to show off. Knox had sensed he was lonely inside and instinctively began to be friends with him, until in their second year they began to room together.

"You made these last three years for me and I'm not forgetting it. Some day you may realize that I've tried to prove I appreciate your friendship."

"Thanks, Vince."

The urge to help Leon mounted within Knox until at last the commencement exercises were over. His family started back to Santa Ana, and with his cap and robe still in the car, Knox headed toward Aunt Bea's home.

She lived on a steep side street off Beachwood Drive, in Hollywood. Knox parked in her driveway and walked up six steps to ring the bell. Frances Billings, Bea Aldrich's combination secretary and companion, opened the door. Tall and poised, in her thirties, she had been known to get rid of a complete bore in thirty seconds flat. She arched her eyebrows, "Knox! Do you want something?"

"I must see Aunt Bea."

"She's busy and I don't remember your having an appointment."

"I must see her." He brushed past Frances, into the spacious living room with floor to ceiling windows, grand piano and oversized divans.

Frances followed him. "You must be tired. Perhaps if I arranged an appointment for Monday, you'd be in a better mood to talk to Aunt Bea."

"But ----"

A voice came from another room. "Frances, whoever it is, I'll see him."

"Aunt Bea doesn't know how to say 'no'."

Knox followed Frances to the rear of the room, up six steps and paused in the doorway of Aunt Bea's study. He had never been in the room before, but disturbed as he was, he felt its restful beauty . . . the book-lined walls, white drapes with tiny blue diamonds, delft blue carpet, desk and chair of white leather, rose leather divan, white coffee table inlaid with iridescent seashells.

With a smile that instantly made Knox feel welcome, Aunt Bea said, "I'm delighted to see you! What's troubling you?"

Frances left the room. Knox slumped into a chair. It helped even to look at Aunt Bea. Her smile invited him like an easy chair. Hopefully he put his gnawing problem into words. "How does one know the will of God?"

"What has challenged you?"

"You remember the Easter retreat when I gave my life to God? Prior to that, because it seemed the right thing to do, I accepted a job as coach at UCLA. Since that I've met Leon ------" He told about the boy, concluding, "I don't know what I want to do. Only being a coach doesn't seem important any more. I want to work with boys like Leon."

"How?"

"I don't know. I do know that merely telling them the facts of the Gospel isn't enough. Neither is entertaining them as some boys' clubs do. It has to be both. But before I do anything, I have to know if God wants me to do it."

Aunt Bea rose from her desk and sat on the rose divan, nearer Knox. "I believe He has His special purposes for each of His children. However, one of the most abused things in the world is this matter of God. Men have committed murder and said God told them to. You will find that not every man who loudly proclaims he is doing God's will is living a godly life."

"Perhaps that's what is troubling me." He had a childhood memory of his uncle, in bare feet, preaching on busy street corners. Gramps said, "If he had to lose his mind, I'm glad it was on a clean subject like religion," and put his son in an institution.

But Knox knew that ever since then he'd been afraid of being a fanatic.

"I believe we can know the will of God. Spiritual leaders say that we can know it from His Word." She picked up a white leather Bible and extended it toward him. "But only the general principles. From it you know it is God's will for you to help others, but not that you should help this Leon."

"That's for sure. How do I know if delinquent boys are my problem? I'm afraid if I change my plans, I'll disappoint Joan."

"After you know God's general principle, there is God's providence. It is more logical for you to help Leon than someone you don't know. We have to accept the circumstances of our lives as being allowed by God. However, one has to be careful about taking guidance merely from happenings. That can become fatalistic. There are also things which can go wrong, lack of funds, misunderstanding of motive. Do they mean we shouldn't go on or that we should fight harder? True guidance is deeper than circumstances."

"What is it?"

"Guidance is of the Spirit. It is found by being quiet before God until you know God's purpose for you."

"Being quiet before God!"

"Exactly! And if you decide God would have you help those boys in the Valley, come see me. Maybe I can help you."

"Thanks." They talked for a few minutes longer before he left. As he walked down the outside steps, he looked up at the stars and thought, *I've got to know You better.*

In the days that followed, he had the edgy, waiting feeling he always had before a race. He moved back home to Santa Ana. Vince moved with him, planning to stay until he found a suitable bachelor apartment near his new job. Knox spent all the time he could with Joan, helping her plan for the wedding. But even as he watched the happy light in her eyes, he knew, *This isn't the main event.*

Each morning he woke before Vince or the rest of the family were stirring and went into the living room. There, he read the Bible and prayed, learning to be still before God.

The conviction grew within him that he had to see Leon again. The coming week was crammed full. The wedding rehearsal was set for Monday morning. Wednesday was Ben and Alison's wedding at Olvera House. Thursday would be his own wedding and the reception. He and Joan planned to go to Santa Barbara for the night, and the next day head for Yosemite and the national parks trip. If he were to see Leon, he must do it at once.

10

"Circumstances form the character; but like petrifying waters they harden while they form."

L. E. Landon

The wedding rehearsal was a mixture of Florence's bossing, Joan's pretty seriousness, and the tittering excitement of the wedding party. To Knox, it was the promise of a tomorrow, when the excitement would be over and he'd have Joan to himself. But afterwards, he refused to go home with Joan and instead drove to the Valley.

At the Nyes' home, he knocked, but there was no answer. Disappointed, Knox walked back to his car, and leaned against it. *What'll I do now?*

"Hi, Champ," someone called.

Knox swung around and saw Leon, carrying several sacks, walking toward him.

"I thought I was never gonna see you any more, what with the wedding and stuff."

"I wanted to see how you were getting on before I went on my honeymoon."

"I'm having a party at my friend's." He held up the packages. "Join us."

"Sure," Knox took one of the sacks and followed Leon down the block to a box-like shack on the back of a weed-covered lot.

Leon kicked open the door and they stepped inside. With a quick glance Knox took in the mustard colored walls, the round oak table, the divan with the cotton matting sticking out of the arms, and the expensive, twenty-one inch TV set.

"This is my friend, the champ, what I told you about." Leon piled his packages on the table. "This is Homer. It's his joint."

"Hi." Homer didn't move his puffy body from the arm chair, but a look of admiration flickered across his pasty-looking face.

"Leon invited me to the party."

"It's Leon's birthday. He can invite anyone he wants."

"And this is Mickey, my girl."

"Lo, Champ." Mickey smiled casually, as if she wasn't too impressed.

"Hello." *If Leon hadn't said she was a girl, I wouldn't be sure.* She was wearing blue jeans and a long shirt and her black hair was clipped short.

Leon began taking the bread, margarine, sliced bologna, pickles, potato chips, cup cakes, and bottled cokes out of the sacks.

"I'll get some knives," Mickey said, and went into the kitchen.

"Help yourself," Leon invited.

Mickey came back with a handful of knives and dropped them with a clatter on the table.

Knox picked up a knife and, frowning at the dried mustard stains on it, decided he didn't want margarine on his bread. He made a sandwich and Leon opened a bottle of coke for him.

After each one fixed his own food they settled down, Knox and Leon on the divan, Mickey on an over-stuffed chair, with her legs over the arm, and Homer in his battered easy chair.

"This is your birthday?" Knox asked. He couldn't accept the fact that Leon's parents were as disinterested as they seemed to be.

"Yeah. I'm seventeen and thought I'd celebrate. And don't go asking me, 'Won't your mom have a party for you?' Because she won't. She and the Old Man are on their vacation and no one told them it was my birthday."

"I see," Knox said because he had to answer, but his sympathy for the boy made him feel sick. He changed the subject. "Did you get passing grades in school?"

"Nope. Teacher likes me too much, wants me to stay around, but I don't think I will. I'm going to get a job."

"Doing what?"

Leon explained his work problems. He had no training, was a year behind in school, and a minor. Too, he wanted to earn a man's wages. "I gotta so Mickey and I can get married."

Mickey threw the crusts of her sandwich half way across the room onto the table. "I don't know that I'm going to marry anyone! I can't see that marriage is all that it's cracked up to be."

"You can't tell 'til you try it."

Knox glanced at the dirty dishes on the table, the soiled socks on the floor, the dust on the TV set, the blanket wadded in a heap at the end of the divan and wondered, "Homer, where are your folks?"

"Hey! What business of yours is it?"

"You don't dig," Leon quickly defended. "Champ ain't no cop. He's my friend. I told you, he didn't turn me in that time."

"Sure, I'm your friend," Knox said. *I've got to be. You all need one.*

"I ain't aiming to go to no juvenile hall. That's a dull joint. This way, I live right, even if my folks is away."

"Away where?"

Homer's puffy body slumped in the chair until it looked like a sack; the mention of his folks took the spirit out of him. "Mom's up north."

"She kept thinkin' folks were going to kill her and went walking around with a knife," Leon explained, "so they locked her up before she stuck it in someone."

"Camarillo," Mickey added.

"Sure." Knox nodded as casually as he could. *I mustn't be shocked no matter what they tell me.* "And your father?"

"He's in the Big House. I guess it's a toss up whether he or Mom get out first, but he gave me money to live on so I stay here. As long as I show up at school and pay the rent on time, no one bothers me."

"How old are you?"

"Old enough to take care of myself."

"But your money won't last forever."

"So what? I swipe what food I can to make it last. Besides,

if I need something, I can go to the man Dad was working for, Orci."

Orci! Knox wondered, *Where did I hear of him before?* Suddenly he was back at Olvera House on Christmas Eve. Alison, with a troubled look on her face had said, "Orci's the scum of the earth. He's a pusher!" Knox took a drink of his coke to cover his shock at Homer admitting his father worked for a narcotic peddler.

"And with his old man gone, this makes a swell joint to hang out in, don't it, Mickey?"

"More or less," Mickey answered, taking Knox's empty bottle. She walked to the table and put both their bottles on it. "I know I wouldn't want to spend a vacation at my own joint."

"What's so bad about it?" Knox asked, trying to size up the girl, who was so tough for one so young.

"You should meet Gram! A whining old beggar, Dad calls her. I guess she is." She went back to her chair and swung her legs over the arm again. "Nag, nag, nag, that's all she does, all day long! She says life ain't treated her first class."

"Has it?"

"I don't know. I guess she didn't have much back on the farm, but plenty of kids. Eight of them. Mom was the baby. She met Dad when he was bumming around the country. They came out here and by the first time he went North, Gram was a widow, so Mom got her to come out and take care of me. I was a baby then. Mom's worked and Gram's taken care of me ever since."

"Her mom works where mine does," Leon added.

"Where did you say your father was?"

"He's away."

Knox nodded. *When they say "away" they mean some kind of an institution.*

"He's where my dad is, at the Big House."

"For working for Orci?"

"Nope," Leon spoke up, "her dad goes in for the most, holding up banks."

"Yeah, sometimes when Dad is home we got plenty. He buys me keen clothes and takes Mom to night clubs, but he don't stay home long."

Depressed by the sordidness of their stories, Knox jumped up and suggested, "Let's wash the dishes."

"They ain't all dirty," Homer answered dully.

"We gotta wash them. Champ is a sucker for washing dishes."

Knox was pleased by Leon's cooperative spirit. He led the trio into the small, messy kitchen with its wooden sink. Finding the soap chips, he helped them wash all the dirty dishes. It was a job. Most of them had to soak because they had been dirty for days or weeks. There was rancid grease in the skillet, and a pile of pop bottles in the corner. Knox said, "Take them back. You'll get enough money on them for another meal or so, and every dime you get helps you to be independent."

"Champ's right," Leon said.

When they finished, Homer ambled back into the living room and half-stumbled into his easy chair. He reached toward the TV set. "Let's see what's on."

"Wait a minute! Maybe I can tell you a story." As Knox sat on the divan he thought of a way he might help Leon and his friends.

"About a sprinter?" Leon asked, sitting beside him.

Knox thought quickly of the Bible stories he knew and answered, "Sure!"

"Then let's hear it."

Mickey eyed the chair where she had been sitting, then sat by Knox.

"If it ain't too long," Homer agreed, and picking up a couple of bags of salted peanuts from the table, tossed one to Leon and began eating one himself.

"This is a story that happened to King David."

"Do I know him?" Leon asked.

"He's the one who killed the giant."

"That's Bible stuff. When I was a kid, Gram used to send me to Sunday school, but she quit," Mickey said, frowning.

"Why?"

"Said they weren't teaching me right, like she learned back home."

"Anyway, David killed the giant and fought a good many

battles until he became King of Israel. He had a son named Absalom, whom he loved."

"Absalom!" Homer said. "Those guys have funny names!"

"And after a battle, Absalom died."

"What's that got to do with a runner?"

"Ahimaaz was a runner and he wanted to run and tell David about the battle, but Joab, the general, said 'No, you shall not go because the king's son is dead.' Instead, he sent Cushi. But Ahimaaz wasn't happy, he wanted to run too and insisted and insisted until Joab let him go. Ahimaaz was a fast runner and he outran Cushi, reaching the King first. David asked him, 'What's the news?' Ahimaaz was out of breath but he managed to gasp, 'When Joab sent me I saw a great tumult but I don't know what really happened.' "

"The dumb cluck! What's the use of running if he didn't know what was up."

"That's it, Leon, and in a lot of ways, what's the use of living if you don't know why you're living?"

Leon, Homer and Mickey stared at him.

"If I come out and have a Bible class so you can learn what life is all about, will you come?"

Mickey's thin face grew serious. "It wouldn't hurt us none."

"And will you show us how to sprint?"

"Sure," Knox promised, happy at their response. "We'll have a full program of sports all summer long."

"I might watch," Homer said.

"Where'll we have it?" Leon asked.

"I don't know," Knox admitted, "but there must be some place." He talked with the three of them and excitedly they made plans for sports, picnics and Bible study. *How eager they are to have someone interested in them!* "I'll see if I can work something out and let you know."

"After the weddin'? That's a long time," Leon said disspirited.

"I might have known there'd be a joker someplace," Mickey said disappointed.

"I'll see," Knox promised. *It'll mix up everything, but I've got to help these kids.*

11

"Resolved to live with all my might while I do live,
and as I shall wish I had done ten thousand ages
hence."

Jonathan Edwards

At dinner that night Knox told his family about the day's
experiences, then he out-sat them until they all went to bed and
he could be alone. He turned off all the lights but one and sat in
his grandfather's chair near the window. Taking Grandpa Mac
Laren's Bible off the bookcase, he read in the Psalms until he was
sure everyone was asleep. Then he knelt, burying his face in the
old armchair and prayed in fumbling sentences.

"I've got to help Leon and his friends. But what would Joan
think? She didn't like my sending the money to Redl. But, Lord,
I've got to give up the coaching job and devote my time to Leon
and the others for You." A feeling of peace filled him and he
realized, *This is how you know what God wants you to do.* You're
quiet inside. He stood up and stared at his trophies and Olympic
medal on the bookcase. *Dad will be disappointed but I must tell
him first thing tomorrow.*

In the morning, there was the usual breakfast that Bull insisted his family eat: sauerkraut juice, cereal with wheat germ and
honey, milk but no coffee, and vitamin pills. Knox kept himself in
check until Vince stood up and said, "Excuse me, but I've got to
get to the salt mines before the boss does."

"Wait a sec. I've something to say about those kids I was
with yesterday."

"I feel it coming! He's going to be a saint!" Vince said dryly, standing behind his chair.

Everyone else stared at Knox. Bull wadded his paper napkin into a ball.

"It's easy for Vince to joke, but I've decided to resign at UCLA and devote my life to delinquents."

"That's a worthy decision," MacLaren said in an assuring tone of voice.

I knew he'd back me. He's living with us today because he spent his money helping stray boys.

Bull scowled at his father-in-law. "You stay out of this!"

And he will. He's always conscious of the fact that this is Daddy's home.

"Those fellows sounded old enough to look after themselves," Stuart said.

"They would be if they'd had our training," Knox tried to explain patiently. "But they didn't have, so they're wrecking other people's property and their own lives as well. Someone's got to take an interest in them."

"You always did have a strong sense of social justice," Lelia smiled. "He gets it from you, Father. Remember the time he took the crippled boy to camp with him? I'm sure if you want to be a minister your dad and I will help you."

"Is that what you want?" Bull demanded.

"No That would mean going to seminary for four years and I don't want to preach. I want to run a boys' club."

"No!" Vince exclaimed. "See you when the storm's over." He walked out of the room.

"Who's backing you?" The veins stood out on Bull's forehead until they looked as they would burst.

"I haven't got that worked out yet." *Dad will never understand. He's been out to win games too long to understand anything but success.*

"But you can't do it. You'll never have another opportunity that pays like UCLA. Don't be foolish."

"Do you think it's foolish to serve God?"

"There are plenty of ways to serve God. Don't I serve Him?"

"In a way, sure."

"Also, I take care of my family. Maybe we don't have a gold-plated Cadillac, but you haven't wanted for track shoes."

"What does Joan think of your plans?" Lelia broke in anxiously.

"I haven't told her yet, but she'll be behind me."

"Don't be too sure! Women have a habit of eating and wearing clothes." Bull stood to his feet. "I give you fair warning, if you don't get on the starting line with UCLA, I won't give you one cent."

Lelia, Gramps and Stuart looked at Knox, silently pleading with him not to cross Bull, but he persisted, "I'm going to talk to Joan."

"Maybe she can talk some sense into you!"

"We'll see."

Within ten minutes Knox was speeding along the freeway toward Pasadena, thinking, *Dad isn't called "Bull" for nothing. He's bull-headed in his determination to make both his teams and his family winners.* Knox remembered that during his freshman year in high school when he decided to go in for track instead of football, Bull had refused to help him. He had to get a paper route to pay for his equipment, until he won at Fresno. Then Bull backed him.

When he decided to go to UCLA, Bull had wanted him to go to his alma mater. That freshman year, only Knox's job in the publicity department enabled him to stick it out. But when he made the Olympic team, Bull had to be in on that. And Knox knew, if he bucked Bull, again, he'd have to prove himself before his father would help him. He might have agreed to his being a minister. A minister had standing in the community, but a boys' worker without a salary — well, Bull couldn't see him doing something that he'd be embarrassed to tell to his friends.

As Knox neared Pasadena, he realized he had nothing to offer Joan and her family either, so he decided to see Aunt Bea first. *She said to come to her if I decided to work in the Valley.*

He by-passed the clover-leaf turn-off to Pasadena and drove onto the Hollywood Freeway. At the Grower Street ramp he turned up Beachwood Drive, to Aunt Bea's, where once again he had to argue with Frances to see the busy woman. But Aunt Bea was gracious as always as she sat on the divan beside Knox. "What's troubling you?"

He told her of his decision to help Leon, then said, "But I have scores of problems. For one thing, what about my lack of Bible training?"

"You've a trained mind, and excellent lesson material is available. You can use it, the same as any Sunday school teacher does."

"But how can I work with the boys and support myself?"

"I didn't tell you before because I wanted you to make your own decision, but for over a year I've been praying for a man to be interested in that section of the Valley. Despite the growing industrial expansion and housing units, there is no local church work among the boys and girls. Perhaps we can work together."

"How?"

"I own a house in that district. I built it, thinking to live there, but my interests grew so I moved in here. It has been vacant about two years, the windows have been broken by vandals, but you and Joan can have it, rent free."

"Then I am right! Isn't your helping me a sign that I am in God's will?"

"I think so. The ways of God are past finding out, but I have noticed that when He speaks to a man, He gives him some encouragement, and then the struggles begin. It won't be pleasant to take a bride to a rundown house. And you'll have to raise your own support."

"Dad won't help me until I prove the worth of my work."

"You'll find that many others take that same attitude." She leaned forward, an earnest look on her face. "I want you to remember what I'm going to say for the next five years. Our God is a God of law and order. Just because you are going to serve Him does not mean that He will break his laws of growth and development. You will face exactly the same problems and experiences that any man does when he goes into business for himself."

"But God is my partner!"

"Exactly! And as a partner He'll do many things for you, but don't expect Him to do everything."

"Thanks." He stood to his feet. "And now I must see Joan and tell her my decision. At least, I have a house to offer her."

Aunt Bea looked thoughtful. "I hope she understands! I have to line up counselors for our boys' camp. I wish you would come. It would be marvelous experience for you. It starts next Saturday."

"I can't. I'll be on my honeymoon then." Knox smiled in anticipation.

12

"Eagles do not fly in flocks."

Unknown

Knox drove up and parked at the VandenBerg's with an uneasy heart. *My timing is bad. A man doesn't change his plans two days before his wedding, but that's what I'm doing.*

He walked briskly up the path and rang the bell. *I must see Joan alone. If only her mother doesn't hang around all the time. At least, Sharon and Pete will be at work.*

Joan opened the door. "Knox, come in!"

It was a delight to see her again, her short tawny curls brushed back from her face, and her hazel eyes bright with happiness. "I've been expecting to hear from you."

He suddenly realized he hadn't phoned her since the rehearsal. He should have called last night, but he had been too engrossed in making his decision. "I'm sorry."

"Mom, it's Knox," she called, and he followed her into the house.

His eyes quickly took in the disorder of the room. Boxes were piled on every chair and on the floor. Across the divan was an array of lace, satin and pearls.

"Come, see Joan's positively gorgeous trousseau!" Florence invited. "I don't believe I can offer you a place to sit down."

"Look, Knox, at my gown." She picked up her wedding dress and held it in front of her, five tiers of embroidered white net, tight bodice with a sweetheart neckline and cap sleeves.

"And she'll wear my pearls," Florence said, picking up the

finger tip veil hanging from a crown. "She has so much more than I ever had. She'll be a positively lovely bride."

"Beautiful!" Knox repeated.

Florence put down the veil. "Will you have lunch with us? We're a little late, but we've been busy."

"Sure. Thanks," he accepted, relieved that he could be alone with the girl he loved.

Florence went toward the kitchen. Joan said, "I'll help."

But Knox caught her hand and held her. "I want to talk to you alone. Joan, you'll always love me, won't you?"

"Silly!"

He pressed his lips against hers, kissing her anxiously. "Honey, you don't know how much I need you. More than ever."

"You sound as if something had happened."

"It has."

As the divan was littered, he dropped onto the floor and pulled her down beside him.

"Mom will think we're silly."

"Let's worry about her later." In hurried sentences he told her of his visit with Leon, Homer and Mickey. "I know that neighborhood is loaded with delinquents, and I have to help them."

"I know you do like to, but you'll be so busy this summer."

"That's just it! I can't go ahead with our plans."

"You what"

"I'm not going to take the job at UCLA. As soon as we're back from our honeymoon, we're going to move into a house in the Valley that Aunt Bea owns. She says it's rundown, but we'll fix it up."

"Who'll pay you?" Joan asked.

"I don't know yet. But something will work out. It has to!"

"But, dearest. You can't turn down a good job for nothing." There was a catch in her voice.

"I have to. You know God's work comes first with me."

"But not this!"

Florence came into the room, saying, "I've fixed us a bite on the lanai."

Joan jumped to her feet and ran sobbing to her mother.

Florence held her in her arms. "There, there, dear, a bride shouldn't cry." She glared at Knox. "What have you done to my Joanie?"

Knox walked over to the two women and though he towered above Florence, he felt like a small boy. "I was explaining to her that I'm not taking the job at UCLA."

"Did you get something better?"

"In a way, yes. I'm going to work with juvenile delinquents."

"Explain to me exactly what you're planning to drag my daughter into," Florence squared her jaw.

Joan drew away from her, and picking up her long white gloves, dabbed her eyes with them.

They are even more upset than I expected. Desperate, Knox tried to explain about the need of the boys, "For someone to care, to play games with them, so by being friends I motivate them to live Christ-centered lives."

"And who will support you while you're playing games with these boys?"

"I don't know, but Aunt Bea has offered us a house."

"It's some run-down shack," Joan sobbed.

"And as my work progresses and people see the value, they will support it."

"You mean, live on charity like the Red Cross? You do whatever you please and someone else supports you?"

How selfish she makes it all sound! "The Bible says 'Seek ye first the kingdom of God, and his righteousness: and all these things shall be added unto you.' "

"I don't think it means putting stray boys ahead of your wife. Surely God expects you to support Joanie."

"I will, somehow."

"You must have some security to offer her. Have you any idea what the catering bill for the wedding will be, let alone the other expenses?"

"I know." *And it isn't polite for me to remind her that I didn't want a big wedding.* "But something will work out."

"There is no need for something to work out. Abandon this

foolish idea!" She put her arms around Joan, pulling her close to her. "Promise me that you'll take the job at UCLA."

"But I can't!"

"Either you take the job, or there'll be no wedding."

Knox's tanned face drained white. "Joan, you will marry me anyway, won't you?"

Joan looked from one to the other. "We have to have some way to live."

"But I know what I must do. I prayed last night."

"I suppose you have a private line to God and know He wants you to put a bunch of hoodlums ahead of Joanie."

"It isn't that, but —"

"Joanie, give him your ring! You should have known when he played the dirty trick he did about the ring, what kind of person he was."

Joan hesitated, then pulling off her ring, held it out, and pleaded, "Mom's right. Unless you think enough of me to keep your job at UCLA, we can't be married."

Knox stared at the small diamond in her hand. He couldn't take it, yet all he could say was, "I have to do what I believe the Lord wants me to do."

Joan threw the ring on the floor, and, sobbing, ran across the room, up the stairs.

"Get out of my house this minute, you cheap lazy, good-for-nothing —" The cords of Florence's neck were taut with anger.

Knox backed toward the door and stepped onto the porch. Florence slammed the door in his face, hitting the tip of his nose.

Feeling bewildered, he walked down the path, got into his car and drove toward home. *It isn't possible Joan and I aren't going to be married. She just showed me her wedding gown. I held her in my arms, with her promise of love in her kiss.*

Where did things go wrong? Joan knew from the beginning I was going to put God first. Or was it as Aunt Bea said, that she didn't understand what she had promised? Numb with shock, he drove home, feeling surely Joan didn't understand fully. He dialed the VandenBerg's number.

Florence answered the phone and when she recognized Knox's voice, said, "So, it's you! Have you changed your mind?"

"I can't!"

"Then Joanie doesn't want to speak to you. Surely you realize what a disgrace it is to Joanie to call off the wedding at this late date. Fortunately she has Sharon and me to help her. Sharon has called all the bridesmaids and I talked to Pastor Degraaf. We told everyone that you plan to put every dirty urchin ahead of Joanie and everyone agrees that she would make the mistake of her life to marry you."

"May I speak to Joan?"

"You may not!"

"Thanks. Good-bye." He hung up and sat there looking at the phone. *If only she'd talk to me!* Desperate, he dialed Aunt Bea and broken-heartedly explained what had happened. She said, "I'm sorry, Knox. Sorry because I understand how you must feel. But also sorry because if you aren't married, you will not be able to work in the Valley."

"What's the score?"

"There will be girls in the gang, like that Mickey you mentioned, and it doesn't look right for a single man to work with girls. People would talk."

"I see," he said. He didn't have Joan. And he didn't have his work either. He buried his face in his hands, remembering how Alison loved Ben and how much she had been willing to sacrifice for him. But when he had been willing to give Joan the consecration Alison had demanded, he had lost her. *It doesn't make sense.*

PART II

JOAN   "Women are like dogs really. They love like dogs, a little insistently. And they like to fetch and carry and come back wistfully after hard words, and learn rather easily to carry a basket."

Mary Roberts Rinehart

1

"Love which is only an episode in the life of man, is the entire history of woman's life."

Madame de Stael

Joan lay on her canopied bed and her heart moaned, *I'm not going to marry Knox, I'm not going to marry Knox!* Her wedding dress, a crumpled mass of embroidered net, lay on the cedar chest at the foot of the bed. *Was it only yesterday that Knox broke my heart? If it takes this long for one day to pass, how can I live the rest of my life?*

Through the long crawling hours she hadn't left her room. Florence and Sharon had been in and out, bringing her coffee or food, asking question after question, telling her what they had told friends. With a few phone calls they had destroyed her dream wedding. *And all those presents. I'll have to return them. The dishes from the princesses! How will they divide them?* Sharon had brought her the newspapers with the column heading announcing the broken engagement of the Rose Queen and the Olympic champion. *It was such a pretty romance.* She remembered how thrilled she had been when he noticed her at the parade, so much so that she had deliberately phoned hoping he'd ask her for a date. And when he had, she changed churches so she could see him each Sunday morning. The proposal by the brookside had been perfect. And now it was all over.

She stared at the underside of the white canopy over her bed. *God, Knox said he had to put You first. Do You mean for him to put some strange boys ahead of me?*

85

She got up and walked over to the glass cabinet with her collection of dolls. On it were a dozen bottles of perfume. In the center of them was a picture of Christ. She stared at it, trying to straighten out her thoughts about God. Pete had always been strict about religion. She and her sisters had been baptized when they were babies. When she was eight, with a solemn heart, she had told the pastor that she loved the Lord Jesus and he had allowed her to join the church.

In those days she had felt the Lord was interested in everything she did. She prayed earnestly that she might be pretty so her mother would be pleased. And that her dad would make enough money to pay the bills so her mother wouldn't fuss.

Somehow, as she grew older, though she still went to church, she prayed less and less. God seemed farther and farther away. She stumbled back to the side of her bed, knelt and sobbed, "Heavenly Father, I love Knox. Please give him back to me."

There was a low rap on the door. Joan dried her eyes on the tufted spread and waited. *Maybe I won't have to answer.* The rap came again. With a sigh that shook her slender body, Joan rose to her feet and opened the door.

Pete was standing there, in his khaki shirt and pants. She hadn't seen her father since she'd broken her engagement to Knox. But now, obviously, he had come home early to see her. "Oh, Dad, come in."

She sat on the cherry-pink chaise lounge and watched him. He stared at the billowy wedding dress, then sat on the slim legged chair in front of the pink-flounced dressing table. *He looks out of place in my room, in all the house! It's Mom's house!*

"I want to talk about Knox."

"Is there anything else to talk about?"

"I like him. He's real."

"Real?"

"Do you realize what an interest he's taken in my camellias? Talking to me about them whenever he's waiting for you? And it isn't an assumed interest to please a prospective father-in-law, but real interest."

"I hadn't realized that you and Knox were friends."

"And he has a real interest in boys, wanting to help those who can't pay him."

"But he doesn't want me," she choked.

"I wouldn't say that." Pete leaned forward. "He can't help wanting you and needing you. For a woman's love, many men give up their dreams. But not Knox, and you mustn't insist that he does."

"Why?" she stared at him.

He could not answer her. For years he had kept his thoughts and feelings to himself. He wanted so much to make her understand how he felt, but all he could do was sit there with his thoughts going round and round.

. . . We Dutch are a solid race. We have given to the world one expression, "Dutch treat." It does not mean that like the Scotch we're stingy. Rather it means you pay your part, and I'll pay my part. We're honest, hard-working people with a religion heavy on theology. Calvinistic. Man is saved by the sovereign grace of God. We have not been a strong missionary church. The Dutch came to America for the business of making a living. The church didn't send out its first foreign missionary until 1920.

. . . Yet always there are those who long to know God and serve Him. As I did in my teens. I wasn't sure how I would serve Him, but I knew I didn't want to be a builder like Pa. How hurt he was when I told him, but he gave me ten dollars. Maybe not much, but a lot for Pa. I made it last me while I worked my way to Los Angeles and then there was the day that, as I walked along the street, I saw the sign, "Bible Institute." Just a small school connected with a church, but those were soul-satisfying days. In the morning, studying the Bible, in the afternoon, working as a bus boy, and in the evening, arguing with the other students, the free will of man versus the sovereign will of God.

. . . I might have gone far for God, only there was the Sunday school class with Flo as one of the pupils. She had the most beautiful skin I'd ever seen on a girl, white with a faint pink flush.

. . . I suppose it was she who got her parents to invite me to their apartment for dinner, often. Afterwards, while they did the dishes, I stayed with her in the living room, listening to the radio. Flo fussed with the dials, always trying to get the station clearer, wishing they had a better set. Then came the day when I caught her hands in mine and asked her to marry me.

. . . That night, alone in my room I faced the responsibility of supporting a wife, but most ministers were married so there must be a way. I didn't realize Flo's capacity for crystal, brass andirons and unit heat. How it hurt the first time I saw her cry. We were talking about the wedding, when she began to sob. I held her in my arms and begged her to tell me what was wrong. She said her parents were objecting to the cost of the wedding she wanted.

. . . I had to make her happy. So I quit school to earn money for Flo. Soon, I would go back to school. Only instead, the years went by too soon, there were doctor and hospital bills for Gloria. Then we moved into an unfurnished apartment and bought furniture. Before the furniture was paid for, there was Sharon and my poor Joan. By that time Flo picked out this house. It is too much to explain to Joan.

Aloud he said, "I gave up my dreams for your mother, trying to be content with your mother's blueprint for my life. I've done well in business and I've tried to bring up my girls to be good Christians."

"But, Dad, Mom's a Christian." Joan was confused. She knew that Florence would be insulted if anyone inferred that she wasn't a Christian, though she only went to church Christmas, Easter and Mother's Day.

"She's a good woman, but she thinks God expects a man to support his wife and children."

"So do I!"

"But is that all there is to a man's life? Must his world revolve around his wife's desires?" He leaned forward, a pleading expression on his face. "Joan, a woman is part of the structure of a man's life, not the foundation — that is his relationship to God."

Joan stared at her father's lined face, and remembered how often when Florence talked of stocking the deep freeze, or lining drapes, he quietly shut off his hearing aid. "You mean that if I could persuade Knox to take the job as coach that someday he would hate me for cheating him?"

"Hate is a strong word!"

"You mean *indifference?"*

He nodded.

"I couldn't stand that! I'm glad Mom couldn't persuade him to change his mind."

"But you sent him away, alone."

"Do you mean I ought to marry him, anyway?"

He nodded.

"Mom wouldn't let me."

"She doesn't have to know everything. That is, not until it's too late to change it. Then she will accept because she must."

"Dad, you're wonderful!" She jumped up and kissed him and stepped toward the phone on the table beside the bed. "I'll tell Knox I'll elope with him. That is, if he still wants me!"

Pete stood up. "I'll go water. If you want help, call me."

"I will."

She waited until he closed the door behind him, then flung herself on the bed. Her hands shook as she dialed Knox's number. *If only Mom doesn't pick up the extension! I hope Knox answers quickly. It's in the hall near his door. He might!* Instead it was Vince who said, "It's your dime."

She lowered her voice, hoping he wouldn't recognize it and asked, "May I speak to Knox?"

"Oh, it's you, Queen! If you want him, wait, I'll get him."

It seemed the longest time before Knox said, "Hello."

"Hello, Knox." *I can't ask him to marry me!*

Again he waited, seemingly endless moments before he asked, "Did you change your mind?"

"Oh, so very much!"

"You want to marry me, anyway?"

"Yes, only —"

"Only what?"

"Dad is willing but I know Mom isn't. Dad thought maybe you and I — and he would help — could be married quietly. That is, maybe we could elope, tonight. You have the license and if we do, I won't have to face Mom."

"Honey, we'll work it out somehow. Only meanwhile, I told Aunt Bea that I'd go to Mountain Top for the boys' camp. Would you mind, too much, if we spent our honeymoon there?"

"Anywhere!"

"Joan, I love you!"

"I do you!"

"We'll work it out together, somehow."

"I know we will." All the ache left her heart. *He loves me and that is all that is important.*

They discussed details back and forth. She still wanted to be married by her own pastor so he agreed to phone Pastor De-Graaf and see what could be arranged.

She hated to let him go but had to hang up so he could do the necessary phoning. While she waited, she hurriedly packed the things she'd need for a honeymoon at Mountain Top. *It'll be as wonderful as any place with Knox!* She dressed in her white frilly blouse, the skirt of her midnight-blue linen suit and her new blue pumps. The phone rang, and she picked it up instantly, afraid Florence might answer on the extension. She had warned Knox not to speak until they were sure no one else was on the line. Hearing no extra noises, she asked, "Knox?"

"Yes, Honey. I talked to Pastor DeGraaf. He says if we come right over, and bring your father, that he'll marry us. I talked to Aunt Bea and arranged for us to drive to Mountain Top after the ceremony, and Vince will be our best man."

She glanced at the clock with the pink angel hovering over it. It was ten after five. "Mom will be in the kitchen and Sharon's not home yet. Dad will help me. I'll make it to Pastor DeGraaf's somehow. I have to make it!"

"Sure you will. Vince and I will leave immediately. And

you'll understand if I'm not dressed up. I have to wear clothes that I can wear at camp."

"Silly! Who cares?" *As long as you're there!*

When she put down the receiver she wasn't too sure she could get out of the house without Florence stopping her. *I can't stand another scene.* She stepped to the window. Pete was watering his row of camellias in their wooden buckets. She waited. *Will he look up?* It seemed an age before he stealthily glanced up. She waved frantically to him. He continued puttering aimlessly about. *Didn't he understand my signal?* He carefully wound the hose in place, gave the nozzle an extra shake to drain it. Then he sauntered toward the house.

Quickly she put on her jacket and slipped a bit of blue straw on her curls.

There was a knock on the door.

She opened it an inch. Seeing Pete, she pulled him in and quietly closed the door. "Knox phoned Pastor DeGraaf. He said if we came right over, and you came with us, he'd marry us. How will I ever get out of the house? I can't face Mom, I can't!"

"You know Flo. When she's cooking, she's busy. I'll go downstairs with your suitcase and get into the car. Then you slip down, go through the lanai and we'll make it."

"I couldn't do it without you!" She kissed him and shoved her suitcase into his hands. He left and she leaned against the closed door, listening to the sound of his footsteps growing fainter.

She waited a few impatient seconds and then tiptoed down the stairs, fearful lest Florence would think of something she wanted in the living room. At the bottom of the stairs, she edged along the wall onto the lanai, then she ran to the waiting car. Pete had the motor running, but he drove slowly out of the driveway, explaining, "So as not to attract attention."

Only when they started down the street toward Pastor DeGraaf's house did Joan laugh. "It's silly! Looks like instead of not marrying Knox, I'll marry him a day sooner than we planned!"

2

"A woman's lot is made for her by the love she accepts."   *George Eliot*

The fear that something might happen again and snatch Knox away didn't leave Joan until they were married and in his car headed toward San Bernardino. Then she sighed with relief. "The last couple of days have been a nightmare."

He nodded agreeingly. "Tell me, how did you live through them?"

She told him about staying in her room, the feeling that she could never face her friends again, of Florence's raging anger, and Pete's encouragement.

"Odd, it's your mother, but my dad who objects to my plans! He had Gramps spend the day getting refunds on our honeymoon tickets. He won't even discuss my decision with me, but Mom's for my doing whatever will make me happy. By the way, when I phoned Aunt Bea that you were coming with me, she said that you'd have to take charge of the soft drink stand. They have no room for the beautiful but idle."

"Sell candy and cokes!" *What kind of honeymoon is this?* "All right, I'll do it."

"I knew you would. I'll have to be with the boys much of the time, but it'll be good knowing you're backing me."

"Knox, you're wonderful!" She leaned her head against his shoulder. He drove along silently into the night. Most of the cars seemed to be going away from the mountain. Mile after mile passed. "What are you thinking?"

"I was thinking it was strange that we were married tonight. Vince and I were supposed to go to Alison's wedding. You remember, I told you about her."

"I remember." Joan moved away from Knox. *Why does he think of that other girl when he's married to me?*

"I thought it was odd that she and I were both married to someone else on the same night."

"Sorry?"

"Who's silly now?" He squeezed her hand and Joan was happy again.

It was after midnight when they arrived at Mountain Top Camp. Knox had to wake up Brewster, the young handyman who slept behind the office. Sleepily he took them to an empty cabin off from the main buildings. "Aunt Bea phoned to give you this. It isn't one of the best, but it's off by itself."

After he left Joan glanced around the cabin with its board walls, two cots with thin mattresses, plain table and one straight chair. "Looks as if our being alone is the cabin's only good point."

"One can't expect much at camp, but we'll fix it up." Knox shoved the cots together, turned the mattresses and went to the car for the bedding his mother had sent. Joan was thankful for the obviously new yellow sheets, yellow polka dot pillow slips and fluffy blue blankets. "Your mom was wonderful to send such pretty things."

"Mom wants us to be happy."

"We will be." *It is enough to be with him,* sang the refrain in her heart.

The strangeness of the place, the thin uncomfortable mattress made her wakeful. Several times during the night she woke up and listening to his even breathing, told herself, *We'll have a happy home together soon. These boys can't take all his time. He'll see the need of a steady job, like Dad and his dad have.*

When she awoke, she was alone. *Where's Knox?* As she dressed she kept glancing out the door. *What could have happened to him so early?* At last he came back, his face glowing, and he was carrying his red Bible. She asked, "Where were you?"

"Alone with God, Honey. I'm sorry if I frightened you, but I have to do that, every morning."

"Oh!" *That's what makes Knox different!*

That day and the next were a wonderful dream. But Saturday morning Joan stood in front of the office building, watching Knox drive down the road to pick up Homer and Leon. *I had him almost to myself for two whole days and I want him for a lifetime!*

She busied herself, with Brewster's help, arranging the supply of candy and soft drinks for the snack stand. When it was all done, she washed and set her hair, wanting to look her prettiest for Knox. She was back at the office by the time he drove up. With him was only one boy, though. With a doting smile, Knox reminded, "You know my pal, Leon."

"Yes," she smiled. She hadn't been impressed with Leon at Gloria's. And she certainly wasn't now. He was a most ordinary boy, in soiled cords and T-shirt, with mussy, too long hair.

Knox helped Leon get settled, then came back to his own cabin. He held Joan in his arms. "Have I been gone one year or two?"

"Three! But I thought you were going for two boys?"

"Homer wouldn't disturb himself enough to come. There's a sluggish retreat to that boy that I'm afraid of. You know, you can't help a boy unless he wants to be helped."

"I'm not a boy, but I want you to help me!" She pressed her lips against his. *If only I could stay in his arms forever!*

But there were always interruptions, including the arrival of Aunt Bea and Frances on Sunday afternoon. Only once was Joan alone with Aunt Bea. She put her arms around Joan's shoulder and said, "Cherish him for what he is. He has a oneness for others that few possess, and the world needs those with his concern."

"I do," Joan breathed with the solemnity that she had when she said her vows in Pastor DeGraaf's living room.

It seemed as if the only time Joan really saw Knox was at

night. After he checked the grounds to see that the last straggler
was in his bunk, he'd come to their cabin, eager to be with Joan.
In her pink quilted robe, she sat on the bed, her back against the
wall, while he sat on the foot of the bed, his hand caressingly on
her foot, telling her the things he had planned with Aunt Bea.
"She says I must stress sports, that's my 'in' with the boys. If I
build up a team, they'll invite their friends to join."

"But if you spend all your time with the boys, how will you
earn a living?"

"The Lord will take care of that. Besides, I have one pledge
from Vince."

"Oh!" *But it can't be much to live on.*

"Aunt Bea says as soon as possible I must get the boys into
a league. Maybe the 'Y'. She has contacts. I think she has contacts with every church in Greater Los Angeles."

Joan pulled her fine-lined eyebrows together. *Why does he
have to make all his plans with Aunt Bea instead of me?* She
offered, "I'll help you."

"I'm counting on that. Are you a good cookie maker?"

"Mostly ice box cookies for teas."

"We'll need the big flat raisin cookies for boys."

"Fancy ones are more fun, but I'll try," she agreed, because
she wanted so very much to be a part of him. "I've read in the
papers that these boys do such crazy things — like releasing brakes
of cars set on hills. Why?"

"Their motivation is complicated. Most of them are im-
pulsive, not given to thinking, and they do things to be noticed,
anything!"

"You could work with much nicer boys."

"Sure, but God —"

But God — Joan wanted to see God's hand in her life as
Knox did, but a bunch of noisy boys didn't seem very holy to her.

On Thursday night of the second week, she waited and
waited for Knox to come to their cabin. *He's late!* She curled
her feet under her and pulled her robe a trifle closer. It was
cold in the mountains at night. *I wish Knox would come. Only*

three more days and this mixed-up honeymoon will be over. On Monday we'll go home, and, surely, it won't be boys all the time there.

The camp grew more and more still. The stream gurgled in the distance. She picked up her white Bible and read the twenty-third Psalm. "The Lord is My Shepherd" sounded as if God wasn't strictly on Knox's side, that He might also be interested in her!

She heard the crackle of a twig and looked up. Knox stepped into the cabin, a glow on his face. *I can't scold. He's too happy!* He dropped onto the edge of the bed and took her hands in his. "Honey, you'll be thrilled to know what's happened."

"Yes, dear."

"Leon has decided for Christ. You have to know the boy as I do, frustrated, arrogant, delinquent, to realize how much this means. His dad knocked him about. His mother gave him only animal care. Here at camp, for the first time I've been able to show him the satisfaction of living a Christian life. And when we get back to the Valley, he's going to be my assistant."

"I'm happy for your sake, but —"

"What, dear?" He lifted her hand and playfully kissed her fingers.

"Only I hoped that when we got down to the Valley I'd see more of you."

"Not too much, I'm afraid!" He stood up and slung his jacket on the chair. "Some people might think I'd been neglecting you up here but Leon's decision is God's seal of approval."

Joan said nothing, but inwardly she prayed, *Heavenly Father, You know I'm glad Knox can help Leon, but don't You love me, too? Wouldn't You help us to have a normal life together?*

3

"A hundred men may make an encampment but it takes a woman to make a home."

Chinese Proverb

Joan was sorry for Leon as she sat in Knox's car and watched him walk along the narrow pavement between the rows of quonset huts. His shoulders slumped and the swagger had gone from his walk. "He can't be very happy at home."

"You see," Knox said as he started driving down the street, past another subdivision, "that's why I'm so anxious to get a club started for the boys. Look at these houses! Seems like there's a million of them."

Joan stared at the row after row of small frame houses, painted cream with green trim. "Maybe only a hundred, dearest."

"This shows how smart Aunt Bea is! When the district started building up, she didn't sell. She knew she'd want a place for some sort of Christian work near these homes. But, Honey, don't expect too much of the house! She said the windows had been broken, and that it was dirty."

"I remember," Joan answered, but still hoped, until she stood in front of the narrow house with its porch across the front, set at the back of a weed and cactus-filled yard. As Joan and Knox walked down the cement path, Joan had the feeling, *It'll be just as ugly inside.* On the porch, Knox unlocked the door, and with one swoop, lifted Joan up in his arms.

"Silly! What's the idea?"

"I'm going to carry the bride over the threshold."

She laughed. *I feel so safe in his arms.*

Inside, he set her down and she glanced at the long, narrow room, two stories high, with a balcony across the rear. The sun shone through the broken window panes, the cream walls were dirt-streaked, and there was a film of dirt on the bare floor.

"What about furniture?"

"Aunt Bea is sending some this afternoon, drapes from the church, a stove they don't need, benches, and a divan that will do for a bed. We'll make out. Come, let's explore."

The first floor consisted of the one large room, a nicely tiled kitchen and a small bathroom. Upstairs, off the balcony, was a bedroom and a larger bath. Knox explained, "Aunt Bea planned the house so she could live here and yet have a place for meetings. Downstairs will be sort of public but upstairs we'll have privacy. Like it, Honey?"

She put her hands on the rail and looked down at the empty room. "It's a roof with possibilities. I don't suppose we could afford wall to wall carpeting like Mom has."

"We wouldn't even want it, with boys coming in and out."

"Must we plan everything with boys in mind?"

"What else?" He looked at her questioningly for a second then said, "I'll get our things out of the car. At least we have our own bedding."

"The sheets need washing —"

While she waited for Knox to bring their things, she thought, *If he'll help, perhaps I can make the place livable.* He brought their suitcases upstairs and she began to unpack, hanging her clothes in the roomy closet. He opened his suitcase and threw his soiled shirts on the floor.

"Champ, Champ, where are you?" came Leon's voice.

Joan followed Knox onto the balcony. He called, "What's up?"

"Those guys! What do you think they've been up to? The whole gang is in the clink. An' Homer, he can't afford to have no law get wise ta him!"

"Begin at the beginning," Knox took the steps two at a time. Joan followed him listening.

"It was like this. No one was home at my joint so I thought I'd go over to Homer's. Only he wasn't home either. So I went by Mickey's. And she knew plenty! It seems that the whole gang, Homer, Wes, Buddy, Slim and Topper decided to celebrate the Fourth by declaring their independence from school.

"They broke into the school house and did they wreck the joint! They got into the principal's office and spilled ink on all the report cards. Ain't no one going to know what grades no one got! Then they took the tapes out of the adding machines and slung them from one light to another. And they threw erasers at the bulbs and broke them. They turned on all the water faucets in the rest-rooms and left them running, flooding the joint. Then Homer got into the stuff in the cafeteria. There wasn't much food to eat so Buddy and Slim spilled flour all over the joint, and mixed salt in the sugar. Homer found a couple cases of pop. They drank some and swiped some, and that's where they made their mistake."

Joan dropped onto the lower step, sick at the thought of the wrecked school house.

"How's that?" Knox asked.

"That's how the cops traced them. Homer wouldn't take the stuff to his place. He knew better. But Wes, he's only eleven and he wanted all the pop, so he took some home, and hid it on the back porch. When everyone got talking about the mess at school, his mom thought about the pop and turned him over to the cops. Ain't dames something?"

"And he told about the others?"

"Yeah. He's too little to know to keep his mouth shut, but if he ever gits outta juvenile hall he'll learn. Buddy 'n' Slim will learn him to shut up the hard way. Too bad he's got his second teeth, on accounta the next set he gets, he'll have to buy."

"Come on." Knox started toward the door.

"Where are you going?"

He paused, his face pleading for understanding. "Honey, don't you see, this is my chance! I've got to see these boys and their parents so they'll know someone is interested in them, and the authorities, so they'll know someone is going to help the boys."

"Champ, you're the most!"

"But most of all, I've got to make these kids see that only the Lord can straighten out their lives."

"You're right, Champ!"

He held her tightly for a moment, then followed Leon out of the house. A deep sense of loneliness filled Joan. She wandered about the house, finished unpacking and looked into closets and cupboards. She found a couple of fancy vases in one cupboard, but that was all.

The long afternoon was almost gone when the moving men arrived. They brought in a stove, much too large for the medium-sized kitchen, but didn't connect it. They carried the tilt-back divan upstairs to the bedroom and filled the downstairs room with backless benches and a lectern. The drapes were piled on the floor near the door.

After they left, Joan unfolded one of the heavy velour drapes. The lining was covered with dust, and there were wide stripes where the red had faded to pink. Tears of disappointment came to her eyes. *Why didn't those boys wait until we were settled before they broke into the schoolhouse? I need Knox today.* She dropped onto a bench and burying her face in the musty drapes, began to cry.

There was a knock on the door. She dabbed her eyes with the edge of her skirt and opened the door. Pete was standing on the porch. "Dad!" She threw herself in his arms and started to cry again. He patted her back, "There, there, Joanie, I wouldn't do that."

"He's left me to go after some crazy boys."

"Tell your dad all about it."

They sat on one of the benches while she told him how Leon had come for Knox. "And he left me, even though he knew I needed him."

"I wouldn't say that!" Pete looked around the large room, with the benches piled hit or miss. "While it's still light, we'll straighten this out, then we'll go over to Gloria's for dinner."

"How did you know where to find me? I didn't know any address to put on my card."

"I called Miss Aldrich and she gave me the address, so I took off from work and came out."

"Dad, you're wonderful!"

"Less flattery and more work out of you."

They placed the benches in even rows and as they worked, Joan asked, "How's Mom?"

"Brokenhearted! Says it's all my fault. But, Joanie, don't forget, you're the baby. She loves you. Why don't you come over tomorrow?"

"I will. All the time up at Mountain Top I worried about her."

"And you'll want to get your wedding presents. Flo has them stacked in your room. That pile of stuff will give anyone a start."

"I hope lots of people gave me sheets." She tried to remember, but it seemed to her that most of the presents were vases, silex coffee pots, lace table cloths, carving sets or casseroles. "Too, I want to get the rest of my clothes."

"Anything in your room consider your own," he offered.

"I'll only take my personal things. I won't want Mom to know how little we have. I don't want her to come here until the window panes are in and things are straightened out."

"I'll send a man out to put in the windows."

"You're going to encourage Knox to chase around with those boys instead of taking care of his own home?"

"I wouldn't say that!"

"Dad, you're old-fashioned, like gold."

"There, there now, it's time to eat. Let's head for Gloria's."

"All right."

They left a note for Knox on the door and drove over to the Walkers' home. It seemed wonderful to be at Gloria's. Joan set the table, walking back and forth from the kitchen to the dining room, while Gloria watched the lamb chops on the broiler, and made tossed salad. Gloria told her of their friends' mixed reactions to the elopement. Joan carefully told the pleasant things about the honeymoon, the present from Aunt Bea, the kindness of the Brewsters and the Donaldsons.

Meanwhile, Pete phoned home and talked to Florence. After a long time, he called Joan to the phone. It was wonderful to hear her mother's voice. Florence wept and scolded but made Joan promise to come see her the next day.

By that time dinner was ready. When the Walkers, Joan and Pete gathered around the table, Joan explained, "All I want is a home as nice as yours!"

"Nice things cost money these days," Harvey said.

"Knox will get them for me."

"Meanwhile," Gloria spoke up, "he's apparently busy. How about my coming by for you in the morning and taking you to have the gas and lights turned on? Then we'll go home and pick up a load of your things."

"All right."

"Me, too! See Knox," said Susan Marie.

"Yes," Gloria promised. "Even at her age, they go for broad shoulders."

Joan laughed but she wasn't quite happy with their plans. *I want Knox to do things for me, not Dad or Gloria!*

After dinner, Joan and Pete went to the supermarket, buying candles and supplies. And as they drove toward the house, she hoped that Knox would be waiting for her. *That'll show him not to leave me. I can go some place, too.*

But the house was empty. She lit the candles, put them in the tall silver candlesticks Gloria had loaned her and Pete helped her put the staples in the cupboards. When they finished, he said, "Joanie, I've always tried to protect you and it's right that I should. But things will be different now. Knox is a good man but he's going to be busy so you might as well get used to taking care of things."

"All right."

"I want to give you a coming-home present. I'll order your phone put in and pay for it for a year."

"Dad, you're wonderful!"

Pete picked up one candlestick and she the other, following

him into the big room. They placed the candles on the posts at the foot of the banisters and sat on the steps. They were both tired and talked in a desultory sort of way, of things she'd bring or wouldn't bring, of what she'd need or not need, of sending the drapes to the cleaners, details that covered her growing anxiety about Knox.

At last she heard his step on the porch and jumped up. The door opened and Knox called, "Joan, Joan. Oh, there you are! And you, too, Pete. Am I thankful to see you! I should have known that if I served the Lord, He'd take care of my wife."

Is he always going to leave me to Dad and God?

"We've been making plans for tomorrow, but perhaps we should have waited?"

"No, do anything you want. I'll be tied up most of the day. The boys are due to appear in court and I have to be there."

"Gloria's going to take me to town so I can have the gas and lights turned on. And then we'll go home and pick up my wedding presents."

"That's good, and explain to your mother that I'll be over as soon as I'm not so busy."

"I will." *But Mom will be offended when you don't come.*

"I'll be leaving," Pete excused. "I'll send over a man to fix the windows and you'll be all right in a couple of weeks when you get straightened around."

"I'm sure we will," Knox said, hopefully.

Knox walked down the path with Pete to his car. Joan, carrying a candle, walked wearily upstairs and started to undress. *He carried me over the threshold and then dropped me!*

In a few minutes Knox came in, and putting his candle on the floor, pulled her into his arms. "I'm proud of the way you've taken hold. You're a winner!"

It's worth it, just for his admiration!

Then he told her about his day. "I went down to Juvenile Hall and contacted the arresting officer. We had a long talk. Tomorrow I'm going to see the Youth Authority officer and maybe the judge. Then this evening, I visited two of the homes.

"Honey, you should see them! Wes's mother is divorced.

She's young, works and tries to bring Wes up right but during the summer she has to let him roam the streets pretty much as he chooses. Then I went to the home of the boy they call Topper. He's the oldest of seven children, thirteen, while the youngest is three. I suppose it's been years since his mother has had any time for him."

Joan sat on the edge of the bed in her pink nightgown. "That other boy, Homer, that you're so interested in. What about him?"

Knox sat beside her, his lean jaw set. "In a sense I'm more worried about him than any of the others. The police aren't holding him, say there's not enough evidence to connect him with the case. But what I don't like is the fact that Orci went to bat for him."

"Orci?"

"He's a friend of Homer's dad, who's in San Quentin. He half-way looks after Homer and I don't like it. He's a pusher."

"A pusher?"

"He sells narcotics."

"How awful! You shouldn't be associating with such people."

"It's part of my job, Honey." He leaned over and kissed her.

4

"Maids want nothing but husbands, but when they have them, they want everything."

Shakespeare

Knox was busy with the boys' troubles the rest of the week. In the end, Wes and Topper were released to their parents because neither one had been in trouble before. An aunt was found to live with Homer. But Buddy and Slim both had long records so they were sent to a detention home. With regret Knox told Joan, "I hate to see them in one of those places."

"What's wrong with a detention home? Apparently their own homes aren't any good."

"Honey, Leon and Homer and the other boys will tell you that those detention homes don't dig. Why, one fellow who used to be a bantam-weight fighter and became a narcotic addict said, 'I learned everything dirty there is to know in a correction home.' Putting a lot of bad boys together is no way to cure them. Even the men who run the homes admit that their prime consideration is to keep the boys locked up."

"They need to be!" *I don't understand his sympathy for these hoodlums.*

"The parents don't see it that way. I've almost made friends with the Nyes. Willie Lou had it in for me because she had to pay for Gloria's paint, but now she's grateful because Leon was with me instead of in trouble."

"On our community-shared honeymoon," she said, her tone of voice betraying her disappointment.

105

He frowned, then glancing around the tidy room, said, "You O Queen, don't need to make a report. I can see the result of your handiwork."

"Thank you, kind sir."

She did feel proud of what she'd done with the house. It was clean. The windows were whole. The furniture was in place. Her presents helped make it attractive. "But we need so many things."

"We'll get them. But now, I've got to get started on my program."

With Aunt Bea's counsel, he planned a full program for July and August for the boys. It was a combination of brains and brawn, with a spiritual note throughout. Joan marveled at the sports Knox had mastered — judo, drilling, roping and the decathlon events. Each morning he held gym sessions in the newly cleaned yard.

Lunch items were charged to Aunt Bea's account at the grocery store and prepared by the boys. On the kitchen door was the list of carefully chosen committees:

"Committee to set out lunch meat: Leon and Wes

Committee to set out bread: Topper and Red

Committee to pour milk: Harry and Ken

Committee to burn milk cartons: Duke and Tom

Committee to evenly divide candy: Shorty and Karl."

It was changed each week and the boys were ready to fight to serve on their appointed committees.

Afternoons the gang would gather in the meeting-room, sometimes only a half dozen boys, other times as many as two dozen. Knox taught them Bible and argued ethics, evolution or sex . . . anything that troubled the boys.

Evening meant another session with them. After the last one had left, Knox would hold long phone conversations with Aunt Bea, or read books on science and the Bible to find answers to the boys' questions. When he did talk to Joan it was about boys — until she never wanted to see another boy.

Mostly, she was lonely. Pete sent money from time to time and Florence phoned her daily, running up toll calls telling her what to do and what not to, but Joan couldn't tell her troubles to Florence. She didn't want her own family to know more wrong things about Knox than they already did.

Neither could she confide in the Taylors. Bull sent them the wedding-trip money for a refrigerator, but otherwise he was waiting for "Knox to come to his senses." Lelia sent them things — a pretty towel or a package of Knox's favorite breakfast food. But Joan didn't feel close to her. Several times MacLaren sent them two or three dollars that he had earned doing odd jobs in the neighborhood, "To help you youngsters get started." And Stuart, now in the air force, seldom wrote.

Joan found her only companionship in the girls who started to hang around the club house. Leon had introduced her as "the Queen, no less" to Mickey. She had shown her admiration by ditching her blue jeans and wearing a dress. She helped Joan with the housework and admired, "You gotta break. Imagine being married to a man who likes to play games in the daytime instead of getting drunk at night like my old man."

"Don't you love your father?" Joan asked.

"How could I love the old man? He don't stay out of the Big House long enough for me to get to know him. Mom drools over him but Gram says that he's a first-class heel."

"Knox and I couldn't have gotten along without our fathers. There must be some good in your dad," Joan defended.

"Gram always says there's two kinds of good. Good and good-for-nothing. Dad's the latter kind."

"Maybe."

Mickey brought over her friends. Billie was only fourteen but already she was bleaching her hair and wearing tight sweaters. And her one black skirt was so tight over the hips that most of the time she went around with the belt unbuttoned.

Her other friend, Gail, had pimples, stringy hair, and had little to say. She was Topper's sister and came to the Taylors mostly because she felt imposed upon at home, where she had to do a large share of the housework.

Joan was sorry for both girls, each in her own way a victim of her undisciplined emotions. And she saw that these emotions were an exaggeration of her own problems. While Billie was crazy about any boy, Joan was crazy about Knox. At the same time she was like Gail, in that she felt sorry for herself.

In September, when school began, for the first time in two months the house was empty of teenagers. Joan reveled in the quietness. Knox busied himself getting the trash burning caught up, fixing the light switch in the kitchen, and rehanging a cupboard door. *It's wonderful to have him to myself!*

She had wanted to have dinner alone with Knox, but felt an invitation was long overdue Vince. He had phoned Knox several times, and dropped by twice, so dinner was a courtesy due him. She used the dishes the rose princesses had given her, and Knox remarked, "Looks like you're going to a lot of trouble for old Vince."

"Unless you count your horde of boys company, he's our first guest," she reminded.

"Seemed lonesome without the gang today. Have you noticed not one of our gang has gotten into trouble since we've been out here?"

"I can't understand why you're so proud that the boys aren't being arrested. No boy should be."

"Don't you know that last year 1,500 juveniles were arrested in San Fernando Valley, or fifty per cent more than the year before?"

"That's a lot." She went into the kitchen, wanting a rest from boys. She was relieved when she heard Knox answer the door and heard the sound of Vince's voice. It was pleasant to serve dinner and be part of general conversation. Until Leon and Wes arrived.

"Time for our meeting!" Knox jumped up from the table.

"You got company?"

"Sure. Come and meet one of the Oympic shotput contenders."

"Another champ?" Leon eyed Vince. Knox introduced the boys, so Joan cleared the table and began washing dishes.

She was nearly finished when Vince came in and leaned

against the stool. "How do you like being nursemaid to an over-grown batch of boys?"

"I like being married to Knox." She always felt defensive when anyone but herself suggested that Knox might be neglecting her.

"He's all that the doctor ordered. But I can tell you a better way to cure juvenile delinquency than Knox's personal boy scout program."

"What is it?"

"Take the parents off the streets at night."

"Oh, Vince!"

"Knox wasn't always heading toward being a saint. He used to be practically normal."

"What changed him?"

"You're asking me?"

Her mind flashed to something she had tried to forget. "It's that girl, Alison!"

"I don't think Knox even realizes it, but he's trying to live up to her ideals for him."

"Why say that to me?"

"Because you shouldn't let him get away with it."

Joan was silent for a moment, hating the thought that the work which took Knox away from her was due to another girl's influence. "Where is this Alison now?"

"With her husband in Mexico City. I'm on their mailing list. They're to study at the mission headquarters for awhile, then he's going into the interior to establish a translation base among the Indians."

"Did Knox ever want to go to Mexico?" she asked, afraid.

"I don't think so. Joan, don't think I'm nosy, but what gives with you and Knox money-wise?"

She leaned against the sink, looking at him. He seemed so prosperous in his freshly pressed suit, new narrow tie and crew cut. "I want to thank you for your checks. They help. In one sense, we have what we need, the house, the furniture."

"Benches, you mean!"

"And streaked drapes. Knox keeps saying that the Lord

will take care of us, but it all goes for the boys and we have nothing."

He put his hands on her shoulders and stared at her, admiringly. "That's what I was afraid of. And things are going to get worse, not better. God helps those who help themselves, so you better do something."

"What can I do?"

"Tell Knox he owes you mink and trimmings. Get him in line before it's too late. This being a big shot with boys can get to be a habit with a man like Knox, who's used to wholesale admiration."

"That's not his motive!" She defended. Even though she was unhappy, she realized that Vince was unjust.

Leon stepped in the doorway and his eyes narrowed as he saw Vince's hands on Joan's arms. "Champ wants you to tell the boys something about shotput. Got the time to spare?"

"It's a deal!" He glanced at Joan and said, "Drop what I said in a well and see how big a splash it makes." He followed Leon out of the kitchen and Joan began making cocoa for the boys, wondering if Knox would ever give her the place her love demanded.

Shortly after nine, Leon and Wes came out and announced that they were on the "Serving refreshments committee." She let them take over, and about an hour later the boys left.

"I must go, too," Vince excused. "It's a neat drive to the apartment and I usually find morning comes too soon."

After fifteen minutes of good-bys, Vince was gone. Joan carried the cups into the kitchen and began washing them. *I'm tired, but there are too many to leave.*

Knox came in and kissed her on the back of the neck. "Did I ever tell you that I loved you?"

"It seems to me that I have a faint recollection. Dearest, please, I want to be serious."

"What's up? Some bug Vince put in your mind?"

"Not entirely. Only, don't you think now that school is started, you might go to work?"

"What do you call the hours I put in with these boys?"

"It's work of a kind," she agreed, looking at the row of cups she had washed, "but you don't get a salary."

"We've managed," he said, picking up the towel and starting to dry the cups.

He's so different from Vince. He sat there and watched me work. She persisted, "I mean I think you really should do something about finances. Don't you ever intend to stand on your own feet?"

"Honey, you don't understand. This Valley is full of boys, and boys between the ages of fourteen and seventeen commit eighty per cent of our car thefts."

"You and your statistics!"

He caught her in his arms, "What's the matter, honey?"

"I think I'm going to have a baby," she blurted out.

"Why didn't you tell me before?"

"I'm not sure. Only I'm getting more and more certain each day."

"That's better news than winning the championship!"

"Then, you'll do something about a job, won't you?"

"Tomorrow we'll go in and explain to Aunt Bea."

She buried her face in his chest, and listening to his steady heartbeat, wasn't too sure that she was happy with his answer.

5

"Early to bed, early to rise
Work like mad and advertise."
Executives' Digest

Aunt Bea, seated behind her desk, smiled at Joan and Knox. "I'm delighted to see you both. I hear from Knox but I don't see enough of you, Joan."

"I don't go much of any place," Joan excused as she took in each detail of the sunny study, the book-lined walls, the rose-colored leather divan, the oversized white desk, the lamp with ruffles of white, rose and delft blue.

"I should have brought Joan in before, but you know how it is with me so busy." Knox sat on the divan with Joan beside him.

"What brought you today?" Aunt Bea asked.

Knox plunged into a detailed account of how discouraged he had been when Leon told him that Wes was pilfering from the supermarket, how he'd talked to Wes and made arrangements with the manager so Wes could work to pay for what he'd stolen. "It was a kindness on the part of the manager because Wes is so small he couldn't do any lifting." Then he told how Homer's aunt had proved to be an alcoholic. "He was almost better off alone."

"The family versus society," Aunt Bea nodded.

Knox smiled, "And that in a way is why we're here today. Joan's going to have a baby!"

"My dear, I'm delighted!"

112

"Knox and I are both happy about it."

"Which brings up the problem of money. I suppose it's an old story."

"It's the usual one. For teenagers the problems are money and courtship, for those in their twenties it's money and marriage, and later it's money and health. But always money!"

"I know I plunged into this work unexpectedly, but I felt the Lord would have me do it. Sometimes, when the boys don't respond I get discouraged, but each morning before Joan's awake I go downstairs to have my quiet time with the Lord."

Joan nodded. *I'll never get used to the queer feeling of waking up and finding him gone.*

"And there I've always found strength to go on. But now —"

"So far we've managed because you and our parents helped," Joan broke in. "But I tell Knox we can't go on like this. He ought to go to work. Even if he did turn down the UCLA job, there are lots of other places he could work. I'm right, am I not?"

"I'm certain you could prove your point to hundreds of people, but, Knox, what did the Lord say to your heart this morning?"

"I know all the arguments are on Joan's side but this morning as I was reading the Bible I came to the verse, 'Be ye steadfast, unmovable, always abounding in the work of the Lord, forasmuch as ye know that your labour is not in vain in the Lord.' "

"So what do you think you should do?"

She's smart. She doesn't tell Knox what to do like I try to do. She leads him to make his own decision.

"I want to go on."

"But what about the baby?" Joan reminded, sharply.

"We'll work something out. I wish it were possible to get your work under the jurisdiction of Grace Church. That's always best. But the board is unwilling to take on any more obligations. The history of the church is that it has lagged behind the need. And the boys of this generation must be reached while they are still boys. Unfortunately, I can't help you any more than I do."

"You do enough with the house and the lunches."

"Do you remember my telling you that you must apply business principles to your work? You have a product to sell."

"A product?" Joan asked hopefully.

"Boys, and their needs, in assorted sizes. This you must bring to the attention of interested people by sending out a monthly letter, telling of your work. You must build up a mailing list."

"I see. I know plenty of people who ought to be interested, such as my friends at UCLA."

"And churches where you have spoken."

"You mean you're going to ask them for money?" Joan flushed, feeling cheap.

"Most missions and charitable organizations run their business this way."

Charitable! The word burnt into Joan's soul as Knox and Aunt Bea discussed what he should say in his letter. Then Aunt Bea said, "You must collect all the addresses you can on 3x5 filing cards."

"And Joan can help me."

The long series of disappointments, the changed wedding plans, the loneliness of camp, the constant flow of boys in and out of her home, suddenly seemed too much to bear. Joan flared, "I won't help you! I won't! And I won't bring my baby into a home that is supported by charity so you can neglect him to pamper other boys."

"Honey, you're upset."

"Let me talk to her."

"What do you know about my problems? You've never been in love with a man who put everything and everyone ahead of you. You've lived in this wonderful home and run everything to suit yourself. I believe in the Lord and that He wants me to have the right kind of a home for my baby."

"Joan, please —"

"Knox, go tell Frances to phone the church office and arrange to have your letter run off on the mimeograph."

Knox glanced from the calm older woman to his disturbed young wife and went out of the room.

Aunt Bea moved beside Joan, taking the girl's hands in hers, and Joan listened, moved while the older woman told her story.

"Each heart has its own bitterness. I remember when I was

your age, living in Boston. My father was a broker and my mother in society. She wasn't merely content with teas and dinners. She interested herself in the local welfare program. She raised money for orphanages and for a home for unwed mothers. She used to visit the girls, encouraging them to find in the Lord Jesus the solution to their emotional problems.

"I resented the time Mother spent with these other girls. I begrudged them a few minutes of kindness. I, who had so much! I took no interest in her work, but much to her dismay devoted myself to dancing, parties, any gay thing that my friends did.

"And along came Austin. Father approved of him because his family had money. Mother didn't like him, said he drove too fast and drank too much, but I was young and determined to marry him. The date was set for the wedding. June twenty-third. I'll never forget the date. The house was full of presents, my wedding dress was made.

"On the nineteenth Austin and I were going to a dance. I lived on an estate a short distance out of Boston. Austin was to call for me. I waited. But Austin never arrived. He had been drinking, started late, speeded, and couldn't make a turn. He ran into a brick wall, and broke his neck. I thought I couldn't live with my grief. I was in bed two weeks with shock. Mother sat by my bedside and read me verse after verse from the Bible. I was torn between their comfort and my rebellion against God for having taken Austin from me.

"Father decided I needed a change and sent me out here. My aunt, his sister, went with me. We came on the train and money went far in those days. I started going to Grace Church. I have no startling climax to my story. Heart-healing is slow, but in Christ I found it."

Joan nodded, admiring the peace Aunt Bea possessed.

"I began studying the Bible, and in time teaching it. My class grew, my interests grew, and I learned one big lesson."

"What is it?"

"To say yes to God."

"Haven't I?"

"Knox is a sincere man and he's doing what he feels God would have him do."

"All I want is to have him pay a little attention to me!" Joan rebelled.

"Joan, I warn you. Leave the man alone! You're jealous of God!"

"I can't be!" *Yet perhaps I am!*

"I was jealous of God's claim on my mother until sorrow drove me to Him. Don't force God to use stern measures with you!"

Frightened, Joan promised, "I won't."

Subdued, Joan went home with Knox. During the day, when the boys were at school, she helped him with his mailing list. She typed the addresses on filing cards, and they had nearly one hundred names on their list. Then she addressed envelopes and put them in shoe boxes on the floor behind the desk. He fussed with his letter, trying to make it say what he wanted it to say. And when he brought the mimeographed letter home from the church, she and Mickey folded and stuffed envelopes.

The response to the letter was as varied as the people who received it. Sharon ignored it, too busy to pay much attention to her sister's unsuccessful marriage. Gloria and Harvey merely remarked, "I hope this will bring in something worthwhile." Pete sent them a larger check than usual. Florence got hold of the one sent to Pete and phoned Knox, scolding him for cheapening her daughter. When she hung up Knox said, "Your mother doesn't understand me, but I always remind myself that I owe a lot to her."

"What?"

"You!" He smiled.

Too, there were wider results. Buchanan of Olvera House phoned Knox, arranging competition games between their teams. Knox received three offers to speak about his work to different church groups. And the young people at Grace Church put Knox on their prayer list. He said, "That's the best answer yet!"

Several members of the Olympic team wrote newsy letters, each enclosing a five-dollar bill. The hardest thing for Joan to take was a letter with a dollar bill from Marilyn Omstead, the girl who had been her strongest competition for the Rose Queen crown.

Joan hoped that Vince would be satisfied that Knox had done all he could. She prepared a speech defending Knox. But when Vince came, he had Sharon with him and said nothing about their former conversation.

Sharon studied the room and decided, "You could do things with this hall if you tried. I could get you some classic oversized sectionals at a discount."

"That takes money and we're fresh out of it," Joan answered, embarrassed.

"Vince, what are you doing Halloween?" Knox asked, and Joan was thankful he changed the subject. "Buchanan has invited our gang to Olvera House for a party and I'd like to accept. It would get the boys out of the neighborhood, but I'll have at least twenty."

"Climbing there, aren't you?"

"More than I can manage myself. We'd need three cars. Harvey has promised to take one load for me."

"I'll help you. Halloween is a dangerous time with boys, let alone potential delinquents. But I don't like your leaving Joan alone."

"She's safe enough," Knox said.

His over-confidence worried Joan and she knew, *Sometimes tragic things do happen to Christians.*

6

"The kindest and the happiest pair will find occasion
to forbear; and something, every day they live, to pity
and perhaps forgive."

Cowper

Late Halloween afternoon, Leon popped in the front door
and called, "Champ, where are you?" He glanced at Joan, then
added, "How about talking to me outside?"

Knox followed Leon onto the porch. Joan heard them talking for several minutes and then, standing at the window, she
watched them take down the athletic equipment and put it into
the basement. When Knox came back in, she asked, "What's
wrong?"

"Just kid stuff! But I'm going to get Vince and Harvey to
take the fellows without me. I'm going to stay here to see that
nothing happens."

"What's wrong?" Alarm twisted Joan's stomach.

"I've known for sometime that there was a gang of hoodlums
who were jealous of our boys. They won't join us because they
won't go along with the Bible part of the program, but they're
jealous of our sports. Leon says he heard that they're using
Halloween as an excuse to wreck our equipment."

"Everything will be all right if you're here," she said relieved,
putting her hand on his arm for strength.

Evening brought a gray fog. Mickey came, bringing with
her Billie and Gail. Joan planned to help Mickey let out the hems
of her two skirts. She was growing tall and her mother couldn't

118

give her money for new clothes. Joan offered, "Maybe I can help you, too, Billie."

"I like my skirts short. Besides, I'm not staying."

"Where are you going?" Knox asked.

"Around." She gave him a wise look and started toward the door.

He strode after her, gripped her shoulders and held her fast. "Something is up some place! Tell me what it is. You know I try to keep the gang out of trouble, that I'm really your friend."

Billie blinked her blue eyes and looked from Knox to Joan, Mickey and then Gail. Gail slouched on one of the benches, and in a dispirited voice tattled, "She's going to Homer's. They didn't invite me, so there must be something up."

"You're jealous, that's what!" Billie yelled and jerking loose from Knox, ran out the door.

"I'm going to Homer's," Knox said, starting after her.

"But we're expecting trouble here!" Joan called, frightened at the idea of being alone with the two young girls.

"You'll be safe. Just keep the front and back doors locked and don't open them to anyone but me."

"I don't like your leaving. You thought it was important enough to stay home from Olvera House," Joan argued.

"Homer's important, too. Mickey, you'll take care of her, won't you?"

"What's up around here anyway?"

Joan anxiously told her of Leon's report of the hoodlum's plans.

"You'll be all right. God will protect you," Knox insisted and left.

Upset by his leaving, Joan with Mickey's vigorous help and Gail's whining, locked both doors, piled benches across the front door and chairs at the kitchen door.

"We'd better switch the lights off. If the boys think no one is home, they may go on their way."

"All right." They closed the drapes and turned out the lights. Joan got pillows from the bedroom and the three of them crouched on the stairs. Mickey chatted about Leon. Joan half-listened, fearful of what might happen. After a while they heard two or three cars driving up and down the street in front of the house, blowing their horns. The "beep, beep, beep" vibrated up and down Joan's spine.

"Is that all they're going to do?" Mickey said with contempt.

"What if it's not?" Gail whimpered.

Several boys stamped onto the porch, pounded on the door, and yelled, "Trick or treat, trick or treat."

"Go away," Gail cried.

"Shut up, you first-class fool!" Mickey said.

Joan pulled Gail closer to her and heard her whisper, "I wish Knox were here. He'd make those boys go away."

"They'll go away in time, and I have an idea the gang really has something planned at Homer's. You know his aunt will be in every bar in town tonight. This is Homer's high moment."

The boys pounded louder and louder on the door and there was a sound of wood splintering. "What's that?"

"Wait!" Mickey tiptoed the length of the room to the front window and peeked from behind the drape. The sound of wood creaking and straining continued. Mickey tiptoed back. "Those first-class heels! They're breaking off the porch railing."

"If only Knox were here!"

The yelling and pounding continued. Joan shivered and held the two girls close to her. Suddenly, she heard Knox and several other men talking to the fellows. Footsteps went off the porch and Knox called, "Honey, let me in."

Joan and the girls hurriedly dragged the benches away from the door. When Knox stepped inside, Joan clung to him. "I'm so thankful you're back."

"I had the police arrest the boys for malicious mischief. I hated to do it, but I had no choice. I was afraid for you."

"So were we," Gail wailed. "I want to go home!"

"I'll take you," Knox offered. "And Mickey, too."

With a sick heart Joan watched him leave again, knowing it was only right that he drive the girls home. She carefully locked the doors, turned out the lights and went upstairs to the bedroom.

She was in bed when he let himself in and came up the stairs.

He dropped onto the edge of the bed and took her hands in his. "Was it bad, Honey?"

"Why did you leave me? That Homer! He's not really one of your boys."

"All the more reason that I have to look out for him. As I thought, his aunt was out, the house was dark but for one small bulb in the kitchen, and full of fellows and girls. I won't go into details but they weren't holding hands. I chased them home, much to Homer's annoyance, but I guess it taught Billie a lesson."

"Why?"

"She had got into more than she expected and was relieved to see me, so much so that after the others had left she showed me where Homer had ditched the marijuana. Homer insisted that he hadn't touched the stuff before and only got it this time to show the others he was somebody. I stayed long enough to destroy it, then came home, saw the gang on the porch and got the police."

"Did you get the police after Homer?" She asked, hoping to never see or hear again of this boy who was always causing trouble.

"No, because I still hope to help him myself."

Joan drew her hands away from his. *It isn't going to get any better. As long as he's in this kind of work, there will be nights like this, or worse!*

Her fear only increased the next day when Knox came home from the police station and said, "The police only kept the boys a couple of hours. Just enough to frighten them."

She looked at the porch rails, split and lying on the ground, and anger mounted within her. "Two hours for all they did!"

"Honey, it's best. Jail never cured anyone. You've got to give them God-conscious motivation. Leon and Duke will help me fix the railing."

"We'll see," she replied, and in the end it was Pete who furnished new railing and two of his men to install it. When the rail was painted, the rest of the house looked so shabby that Pete had his men paint the whole place. Joan loved her dad for his goodness, but it hurt her pride to see him do the things she felt her husband should.

The holidays brought their own problems and hurts. For Thanksgiving both families invited them to dinner. Knox settled the problem of which invitation to accept in typical fashion. They went to neither but had a special Thanksgiving service for the boys and invited Mickey, her mother and grandmother to dinner. Florence simply couldn't understand his attitude, and for over an hour Joan listened to her mother rave about Knox's "utter lack of consideration."

Christmas was an even worse trial. What money they had was spent for the boys and their families, with their own families left out. Joan wasn't sure about the Taylors, but she knew her mother didn't understand!

New Year's brought a flurry of former Rose Queen invitations that Joan was able to accept by spending a few days with her family. Florence bought her new clothes and she enjoyed the excitement of luncheons and dinners. When she came back to the Valley the combination boys' club and home was harder to bear than ever. Knox found her lying on the bed, crying. He took her in his arms. "Honey, what's wrong?"

"When are we going to have a home?" she asked with the desperation of a girl clinging to her dreams.

"This is our home," he insisted, frowning.

"For always?"

"No, someday I hope either to build or buy a really suitable boys' club with a gym and a craft room, and we'll have a real apartment, not just a room for ourselves."

Joan sighed but didn't answer, listening to him plan his ideal settlement house. *He won't change as long as he's in this work. If only he'd work for Dad, we could live with them!* A stark hope was born in her heart, hope that seemingly saw no answer, for each day drove him farther and farther away from her and farther and farther into his work. Nearly every day between twenty and thirty boys came to the house. When Knox wasn't busy directing their sports activities or teaching them Bible, he was counseling them. The boys became a member of an inter-church sports league. Vince came out more and more Saturday afternoons and sometimes on Sunday to help Knox.

Usually on Saturdays Vince managed to get out in time for lunch. They ate at the dinette, slightly behind the stairs, near the kitchen door. The second Saturday in February, Joan served chipped beef on toast and ate quietly while the men talked.

"You certainly have the boys eating out of your hand," Vince said, "Yet you're strict with them. You have rules and mean them."

"That's because no boy really likes to get by with anything. He wants you to demand his best. Don't forget that though man is a sinner, he was originally made in the image and likeness of God."

The front door opened. Joan knew without looking up that it was Leon. Knox said, "I'll be right out." He finished his last couple of bites, then explained, "Leon wants to loosen up his throwing arm before the rest of the gang gets here."

"Hop to it," Vince said. "I'll be out in ten seconds flat."

Knox and Leon went out into the yard. Joan could hear them throwing the ball back and forth. Vince quietly finished his coffee, then asked, "Have you seen the newspapers the last couple of days?"

"No, we don't have one delivered because of the expense."

"But radio?"

"We're too busy to listen much."

"But Knox must have heard." He reached into the inside pocket of his coat and took out a carefully folded newspaper page.

Joan took the paper, glanced at the banner headlines about local politics and then saw the smaller one, Two MISSIONARIES MURDERED IN MEXICO. With mingled shock and surprise she asked, "Alison?"

"Her husband."

She read, "Mexican authorities left yesterday to go into the interior to find the bodies of Ben Moore and Lloyd Hunter. Both men have been reported murdered and robbed. They served under Biblical Translators, an organization which has worked in co-operation with the Mexican government for over twenty years. Moore and Hunter had gone into the mountains to contact a new tribe of Indians. An old woman, a member of the tribe, reported having found the bodies and hiked two days over the mountain pass to tell Alison Moore, wife of Ben Moore."

"How awful!"

"The newspapers and radio have been full of it. Hunter left four children and Alison was only a bride. Married less than a year."

"Eight months. She was married the same night Knox and I were," she remembered grimly.

"The press has been all for the men. Their mission is highly respected, and worked in the country as part of Mexico's educational program for the Indians. The authorities are stirred up over this and will catch the murderers."

"Does Knox know?"

"He must have heard. I can't understand why he didn't tell you. Unless he's too upset!"

She can't really mean anything to Knox! He hasn't mentioned her since the night we were married. Then he only remarked that it was a coincidence that we were married on the same night. He hasn't thought of her for months. Or has he? Her feeling became all mixed up. There was a jealous fear that now Alison was a widow, Knox might regret that he had married her. And she had an uneasy feeling because this girl, who was supposed to be so much nearer to God than she was, was a widow. *Would God let something terrible happen to Knox, even though he is in His work?* Terror gripped her heart as she clutched her hands together.

7

"No child is born delinquent."
*Interim Report on Juvenile
Delinquency by the United
States Senate*

Off and on, for the next couple of weeks, the newspapers and magazines covered the murder of the missionaries. Knox admitted to Joan that he had read of Ben's murder but said that he had hesitated to discuss it with her because of her condition. Now, while Joan sat on the lower stair, he walked the long aisle between the benches and went over his friendship with Alison. "When she turned me down, I asked myself, what are my goals in life? Am I on the winning team? And I decided to play the game with Christ as my Captain."

"So you do all this to please her!"

"Don't get me wrong!" He stopped in front of Joan, staring down at her. "Alison may have set me thinking, but what I do, I do because I believe God would have me do it."

If only I could be sure!

"Why don't you write Alison a note of sympathy and sign both our names?"

"All right." She did write, including a few words of the soon-coming baby. *So she'll understand how completely she's lost him.* Then Joan went back to counting months, weeks, days.

In May Knox arranged for Mickey to stay with Joan whenever he had to be gone any length of time. One day when he went to see the principal about Leon's graduation, Mickey came over as soon as school was out. She asked, "How's things?"

Joan was sitting on the chair near Knox's desk. "It's wonderful to see you. I'm not sure yet, but I think my time has come."

"Ain't that something!" Mickey dropped onto the front bench.

Joan glanced at her watch. "I had a pain about twenty minutes ago. I'm timing them, hoping Knox will be here soon."

"Champ will."

There was a knock on the front door.

"Who can that be?"

"Answer it, will you, Mickey?"

Mickey walked down the aisle and opened the door. "Why Homer, come on in! How's things?"

Homer stepped inside and out of drowsy-looking eyes, peered around the room. "Is Champ here?"

"No, but come in and wait," Joan invited. "He'll be happy to see you."

Homer shuffled down the aisle. *He's lost weight.* He dropped onto the front bench and yawned. Mickey sat beside him. He looked at her as if she bothered him and moved away.

"I don't bite," she said.

"How's school, Homer?" Joan asked, worried by the boy's nervous behavior.

"Who cares?" He squinted his eyes, staring at Joan.

"I'm just interested." *He isn't acting like himself.*

"I'm laying off school. It bothers me, no end." He shuffled toward the window, staring at the near-by housing project. "They build the houses too close together around here."

"Go look out the other window at the baseball diamond," Mickey said. "Maybe that view will suit you."

He crossed the room to the window by the dining room table and stared out.

Mickey gave Joan a wise look and walked casually over to Homer. When she neared him, he jumped as if startled. She said, "I was only going to offer you milk and cookies."

"Who cares?" He shuffled down the aisle and without looking back at Joan said, "I won't wait. It's probably too late anyhow."

"Besides, you need a 'fix,' " Mickey called after him.

He stared at Mickey. "Don't say that!" He yawned and went out the door.

"What's wrong with him?"

"Looks to me like he's on the junk."

"Junk?"

Mickey sat down on the bench. "I've had my eye on Homer for a while. Billie told me about the marijuana he got for the gang at Halloween. Since then I've known he had a connection and sooner or later he'd try the junk. Homer don't like the looks of life, so why not?"

Joan tried to picture what life would be like to a boy whose father was in San Quentin, whose mother was in Camarillo, and who lived with an alcoholic aunt. *Even so, Mickey can't be right!* "Not narcotics?"

"Yeah, little old joy pills."

Pain clutched Joan. She bit her lip, then glanced at her wrist watch. "This must be my time. I wish Knox would get here."

"He's probably gone by Wes's. His mom is sick and you know how Champ is when he hears things like that."

Joan nodded, thankful for the girl in her red-checked dress, with her dark windblown bobbed hair and bright brown eyes. *She's a pretty girl. Yet there's a brittleness about her that isn't normal for a sixteen-year-old.* She thought of Mickey's father up with Homer's father. "What is it they call your father?"

"Speedy O'Brien, because he's fast with cars, women and cops."

"Where did your mother meet him?"

"She was a dumb cluck working at a lunch counter next to a filling station back in Arkansas. He came in, ordered a nickel glass of milk and left a dime tip. She thought he was a big shot. How was she to know he was on the lam?"

Joan had to translate Mickey's slang to realize she meant her father was dodging the police.

Mickey stretched out on the bench, one arm curved behind

her head for a pillow. "I don't think my old man was serious at first. Mom was just another pretty girl and he liked to turn on the charm. When he saw that she had fallen for him he thought he'd better pick up something good while he had the chance. He got her to run off with him and married her. She always has been nuts about him, and in his way he goes for her. It's just he's got the itch to get money faster than he can earn it. He's had a record ever since he was twelve. I'm going to see the school records of any man I marry."

"You know all about Leon."

"Leon's a first-class kid. If he graduates and gets a job, I might marry him but I'm not marrying any guy that'll put my kids in the spot Dad put me."

"Tell me about it."

Mickey looked at Joan speculatively, then decided, "I guess you gotta talk about something until Knox gets here. The earliest I can remember is Mom and Gram living here in California. All I knew was that Dad was away. I was too little to ask questions. I knew that Gram didn't like him and that Mom used to cry an awful lot.

"I was six the first time Dad came home. That was something! He had Mom quit work and they went places. He was good to me, always buying me toys and pretty clothes. I know now he was on parole, but he didn't keep it. Within six months, he was gone again, and Mom and Gram settled down to the old routine. I kept asking when Dad was coming home. And Gram would tell me to shut up. I was ten when he came home again, and this time I knew something was wrong. The cops used to come to the house and take Dad away for questioning whenever there was a big robbery. Dad used to say, 'Don't let 'em get you down. I'll beat this rap yet!' He was the cheerful kind. I got to be like him, cheerful on the outside but all uneasy inside."

Joan bit her lip and glanced again at her watch. "Go on!"

"I was twelve when the big deal happened. Dad and a couple of friends held up a bank. It was to be the first-class job of his life, enough money to buy us a large economy-size world of our own. The newspapers were full of it. The cops came around.

Dad disappeared, and they were suspicious of him. The kids at school would yell at me, 'Your dad's a jailbird, a jailbird.' I got into a couple of fights and then I stayed home. That's why I'm behind in school now.

"Maybe the cops wouldn't have caught Dad, only he sent money to Mom and me. They traced him through the envelope. And then the papers really broke loose. Everytime I walked the streets the headlines screamed at me. And stuff over the radio, I couldn't stand it. The reporters came to the house asking, 'How does it feel to be the daughter of a bank robber?' They got ahold of a picture taken of Mom and Dad when they were first married and printed it.

"The cops caught Dad and put him in jail. Mom used to go visit him. They wouldn't let me see him, but I'd hang around downstairs, walking the corridors of the Hall of Justice, looking at the people, thinking they knew my Dad was up in the jail.

"And then there was the trial. Mom let me sit with the audience and sometimes I could talk to Dad. He had me keep everything there was in the papers about him in a scrapbook, and bring it to show him. He liked all the attention. Me, I just wanted a first-class hole to crawl in, but those reporters don't let no one alone. They were always knocking on the door asking questions. Anyplace I went, people stared at me."

Joan moved over beside Mickey and put her arm around the girl.

"The judge sent Dad away again. I tried to go back to school but I couldn't take it. Some of the kids asked things that were none of their business and real nice girls wouldn't associate with me. The teachers tried to be kind but they ain't like friends. I stayed home the rest of that term. Then Mom moved, got a new job and said I gotta go back to school. I did, but this time I was careful to make my friends with kids of my own kind, like Homer, whose dad knows mine. Since the big mess, Knox is the only decent man that's treated me as if I was like any other girl. He listens to me, wants to be friends, and you, too."

"We do love you." A wave of pity for Mickey swept over Joan but she knew, *Without Knox's driving ideals I wouldn't have helped her. I'd have stayed in my parents' comfortable home and avoided girls like Mickey.* "Knox is wonderful! Only I wish he were here now."

"At least he's not in the Big House."

A pain swept through Joan. "Maybe I'd better phone Gloria." *I hate to call my family at a time like this. If only Knox were here.*

As if in answer to her need, the front door opened and Knox strode in the room. "Hello, girls."

"I told you Champ would get here." Mickey smiled, relieved.

"I think we'd better phone the doctor and get me to the hospital." Joan anxiously told him about her pain. "And they're getting closer and closer together."

He held her in his arms. "I'll phone right away." He went to his desk, called the exchange and talked to Doctor Seymour. When he hung up, Knox said, "She said she'd meet us at the hospital."

"I have my things packed. Mickey, will you run up and get my overnight case in the closet?"

Without a word Mickey ran up the stairs.

"By the way, Homer was here looking for you."

"What did he want?"

"I don't know. He acted so queer. Mickey said she thought he's been taking narcotics. She said he'd had a 'fix.' "

"I must go to him." He started down the aisle.

Joan stared at his broad back, the pain in her body demanding that he stay with her, but her pride sealed her lips.

Then he turned and walked back to her. "He'll have to wait. I have to take care of you."

Joan started to cry. He held her in his arms. She smiled, "You do love me, don't you?"

"Sure! What made you think I didn't?"

"I'm silly."

He took her to the hospital, talked to the doctor, phoned both families and stayed by her side as long as the doctor would let him. She forgot the times she had felt neglected, thankful only for his love. She was thankful, too, for the normal, healthy boy, whom they named Peter, much to her father's delight.

Petey was a delight to all of them — especially to Joan, who, after she got home from the hospital thought, *Knox is gone even more than ever.*

Little Petey was only three weeks old when she stretched out on the bed with him beside her. She was half asleep when she heard Knox's even tread on the stairs. He came into the room and stared down at her. "Honey, did I ever tell you that you were beautiful?"

"Seems like it! A long, long time ago."

He flung himself on the bed. "I get too involved."

She carefully smoothed the lines of his brow. *It's so wonderful to be with Knox.* "You mustn't, for my sake and Petey's."

"Only now things are in a worse mess than ever."

"What's wrong?"

"Homer. I've been over to his place several times of late. And Mickey was right. He's on the junk."

"How could he!"

He sat up, and frowning, explained, "I've been talking to the narcotic detail of the Los Angeles Police Department, to Lieutenant Dawson and Inspector Best. They say that two things are necessary for one to become an addict. In the first place, a person must be what is termed addiction-prone, that is emotional factors make the boy or girl unhappy, seeking escape. Many people are addiction-prone, but find release in other ways. Some become mental patients, others alcoholics, or they find relief in excessive or even escape reading. The damage is done when an addiction-prone person makes a contact with a 'pusher.' That's what happened to Homer. He knew his dad's contact. And now Homer is ruining himself and is dangerous, liable to tempt some of the other kids, as he did Hallowe'en night. I've failed as far as Homer is concerned."

"But you couldn't help it. You tried to help him. Are you going to turn him in now?" She asked, disturbed. She was sorry for the boy and yet it would be a relief if Knox wasn't involved with this worst boy of the lot.

"In a way. That's why I went to the police this morning.

They are going to work with me, and we're going to try to trap Orci."

"Not that man! You mustn't!" she exclaimed, frightened.

Knox's jaw took on a set look. "I must do what I can to stop Orci. Before I went to the police, I went to Buchanan. He told me that Johnny Orci grew up near the Plaza, the oldest of a big family. As a kid he had a bunch of petty thief raps. The same old story — no one cared about him. Then he became a prize fighter with not enough fights and finally was arrested for taking part in a robbery where a man was shot but didn't die. When Orci came out of prison, he started wearing expensive clothes, and being a big shot to kids. But those who were his friends were soon on dope. The police never have been able to get anything on him, because by the time the police know who he's working with, it's too late, the kid's an addict. However, this morning Dawson, Best and I figured out something."

"What are you going to do?" she asked, gripping her hands together in nervous fright.

"Leon is going to tell Homer that he would like to make a 'buy,' that he figures he can sell to several fellows. Then Homer will set it up for Leon to meet Orci. Dawson and Best will tail Leon and when Orci makes the sale, the police will get him with the goods."

"But won't Orci know that you were the one who really trapped him?"

"He may figure it out, but what of it?"

"I don't like it." She listened to Petey's even breathing, and apprehensively repeated, "I don't like it!"

8

"Good has but one enemy, the evil: but the evil has two enemies, the good and itself."

J. Von Muller

Joan, in her robe, leaned over the balcony watching Knox say goodnight to the boys at the door. Wes looked at him with a blind adoration. Topper jiggled back and forth. And Leon stood squarely beside him. *How he's changed from that sullen boy I met at Gloria's!* A fussy wail came from the bedroom. She hurried in and picked up two-months-old Petey. "There, there, I'll get your bottle in a second."

Carrying the baby, she went down the stairs. The sound of Knox's easy laughter drifted across the long room. In the kitchen she skillfully balanced Petey as she took his bottle out of the refrigerator and put it in the bottle warmer.

I wish Knox would hurry! The last few days he had been busy with Lieutenant Dawson and Inspector Best, making plans to trap Orci. Today had been the big day, but when Knox and Leon had arrived home, Wes, Topper and several of the boys were waiting for him. An assuring smile had been her only guarantee that everything had gone as Knox hoped.

The door slammed. Knox's step was light and quick as he strode the long aisle into the kitchen. "Let me hold him." He took Petey from her. "He's getting heavier and dearer every day."

"Look at the example you've set him!" She took the bottle from the warmer and tested a drop of milk on her wrist. Deciding that the temperature was right, she passed the bottle to Knox.

He held the bottle for Petey and she insisted, "Do tell me every-thing that happened."

"It all went according to schedule. Orci was fooled com-pletely because Leon was young and a friend of Homer's. He even arranged for him to come to his home. Leon and I went into L. A. after school. We met Dawson and Best near the City Hall, and then drove to Orci's on the east side of town. We staked out while Leon went in, and when Dawson and Best thought everything was set, they broke into the house. Odd place, looks like a dump outside, but inside there is every possible luxury.

"Orci tried to throw the heroin down the toilet, but Best tripped him and knocked the package out of his hand. He was selling only a comparatively small amount to Leon, but Dawson and Best searched the house and found a half kilo of heroin in a canister marked 'Sugar.' Of course, it wasn't pure. Besides, there was marijuana and a couple of lay-outs."

"What's a lay-out?" Joan interrupted.

"It's what the addicts use to take dope, a spoon on which to heat the stuff and a needle and an eye-dropper that they use for a hypodermic syringe. Pitiful odds and ends. I wish I could show you one."

She brushed aside his explanation and reverted to her fear. "But Orci, did he see you?"

"Sure! I wanted to stick with Leon and we went with Daw-son and Best while they booked Orci."

"I'm glad he's locked up. What did they do to Homer?"

"Poor boy! To the hospital to take the cure. He's got a fight ahead of him."

She took Petey and his bottle from Knox, went into the living room and started up the stairs. Knox walked toward the light switch near the front door. In the tense stillness the ring of the phone startled them both. Joan gasped, "Who can that be?"

"I'll get it." He turned toward the phone on his desk.

"I hope it isn't Mom." Joan waited, carefully holding Petey's bottle at the proper angle so he could keep on drinking.

"Hello. Yes, this is Taylor. Oh, hello. Are you sure?"

Why doesn't he call whoever it is by name so I'd know whom he's talking to?

"I'll be on the lookout but I can't take him too seriously — don't bother to do that." He listened for several minutes. "Sure. Good night."

"What's wrong?"

Knox came to the foot of the stairs and looked up at her. "That was Dawson. He said Orci had been released on ten thousand dollars bail."

"That's a lot of money!"

"Only costs him one thousand with a bail broker. Dawson thought I should know. He said that Orci suspects me of framing him and might come out here."

"Oh, no!" She hugged Petey closer to her. His bottle slipped and he whimpered. She quickly put the nipple back in his puckered mouth.

"They even offered to stake out a man but I told them I wasn't worried. Orci's the kind to talk a lot but he's too yellow to do anything." He started again toward the light switch.

"I wish I had your faith." She went upstairs into the bedroom, settled Petey in his crib and loosened her robe. It was warm and she wished she had a thinner one. *Is there any chance that Knox will think to give me one for our anniversary? Perhaps I should tell Gloria to suggest it to Knox.* The empty bottle slipped from the sleeping Petey's mouth. Suddenly she grew conscious that Knox was talking to someone downstairs. His voice was low but Joan sensed a tenseness to it. And she didn't recognize the other voice.

She stepped out on the balcony and looked down. Knox was standing near the front door with his back to her and his hands stretched above his head. Facing him was a short, stocky man with a hat shading his face. In his hand he had a revolver.

She gasped.

The man glanced up and seeing her, said, "So, one lady! Champ, please back up to the foot of the stairs and you, Señora, will please to join us."

Joan felt the blood drain from her face. Despite his politeness, Joan knew, *That man means business with that gun.* Knox slowly backed up, step by step, and the man with a cocky step followed him. *Perhaps he doesn't know about Petey.* She put her hand on the banister to steady herself and crept slowly down the steps. At the foot of the stairs she and Knox stood side by side, facing the stranger who wore highly polished shoes, a well-tailored suit and a gray felt hat. There was a hard glint to his dark eyes and his narrow chin was thrust forward.

"This is Johnny Orci," Knox said.

"Oh!" Joan shivered.

"It distresses me to inconvenience a lady," Orci enunciated each word clearly. "But your husband has caused me mucho inconvenience today. For a truth, he has made me the inconvenience of a lifetime. For years, I have carefully built up my business, taking care of mucho relatives, my mother, brothers and sisters, and now, in one swoop, your husband destroys everything. Do you know what rap I face?"

"No."

"I have a small record that doesn't help. I could easily do ten years. Maybe twenty. And I'm not going to do it."

"What are you going to do?" Knox asked.

"I'm going to put you where you can't hurt anyone else, and then I'm going East, but it means that I have to make my connections and start all over again. It is mucho inconvenience."

Joan looked at the man's hard face. There was no mercy there. She felt a twisting fear which ran along each nerve across the back of her neck.

With a mocking smile on his face, Orci said, "I hear you are the Olympic decathlon champion. But all your training is worthless when faced with a bullet.

"Señora, I will save you the mucho inconvenience of seeing your husband die. I will let you go upstairs. That also takes you away from the phone. You will stay up there until you count to one hundred. That will give me time to get away. When you come downstairs, your husband will be very, very dead. Yet, I warn you, don't call the police. I need time to get mucho far away. Phone your mother, and if you wish, your doctor. He will be necessary to sign the death certificate. Again I warn you, do as I say, or I will come back and finish you, too. I could do it, that I think I have convinced you?"

"Yes," Joan swallowed.

"Don't be frightened, Honey. There's an answer to this," Knox said in a soothing voice.

"You said Orci wouldn't come but he's here!"

The faint cry of a baby floated down the stairs. All three instinctively looked upward. Orci said, "So, you have a baby! All the better. You will not tell the police your husband is dead until tomorrow, or I'll come back and kill the baby."

"No!" Joan shook with terror.

"Now get upstairs to the baby and let him cry, then you may not hear the sound of the gun killing your skunk of a husband."

Joan looked at Knox. There was defiance to the set of his shoulders and his chin, and a faraway look on his face that made Joan realize that he was praying. *He expects a miracle!* She clung to the banister and prayed, "Lord, help us!" as she started up the stairs.

Someone pounded on the door. Joan stopped halfway up, her heart beating fast with hope.

"Ask who it is," Orci whispered.

"Who is it?" Knox called.

"Lieutenant Dawson. Let us in."

"You make one effort to come in and I'll plug Taylor now," Orci yelled. "Tell them I've got one gun on you."

"Dawson, he's right. He's got a gun on me. Please, go away. Maybe he and I can work this out."

"Okay," called Dawson's voice and there was the sound of footsteps going down the porch steps.

"They don't fool me!" snarled Orci. "They're planning some way to trap me. But I'll outsmart them." He put his foot on the front bench and resting his right elbow on it, kept the gun carefully aimed at Knox. "I have to have a way to kill you and then get away. Let me think."

Petey's cry rose a pitch higher. Orci glanced upward. "We do it with the least inconvenience. Knox, you will talk to them, telling them what I plan to do and that they must cooperate if they want the pretty Señora to live. You will tell them that I have your wife and baby and am using them as a shield with a gun at their side, and that the police must let me get to my car and get away. And that if they put out a bulletin sending other cops after me, I kill both the wife and baby. I'll keep them both with me until I get to where I'm going."

"You can't do that! That's kidnaping!"

"So what? Get enough on a man and a little more doesn't matter. You got me arrested for possession, ruined my business. Now they'll charge me with threatening you, and as soon as I kill you, that's first degree murder, so why shouldn't I do a little kidnaping to keep my freedom? Go, get that baby."

"No!" Joan froze.

"I said go get that brat. I'm killing your husband, believe me. He's got that coming to him, but I'm getting away from this place afterwards, and you and the baby are coming with me, so get the brat and put on a dress."

"No," Joan repeated.

"Señora, can't you say anything but 'no?' Especially when it won't do you any good? Please, go, put on a dress and get the crying one, and if you wish, extra diapers. As long as I need you, I take good care of the baby."

"Go on, Joan, do as he says," Knox encouraged her.

Feeling limp, she went up the stairs and into the bedroom. Petey whimpered. She looked down at him. "Petey, I'll take you up in a minute."

She threw her robe on the bed and slipped on the pink checked dress she had worn that day.

"Hurry up," came Orci's voice. "My trigger finger is tired."

"I'm coming." Joan threw a pile of diapers in a small bag and picked up the empty baby bottle, *I'll need it and the bottles in the refrigerator*. She took Petey in her arms, laying his head on her shoulder, and threw a coat over her arm. Petey fussed as she started down the steps. Orci took his foot off the bench and leaning on the lectern, watched her come down the stairs.

"Let me help her," Knox begged.

"You do it, but don't forget I'm trigger happy, so move toward her, not me!"

Knox lowered his arms and started up the steps toward Joan. Halfway down, she paused, "You take the diaper bag."

Knox reached her side and turned, facing Orci. Joan saw Knox shift his weight, tense his muscles, and then he leaped forward, making a broad jump, landing on Orci. Orci, knocking the lectern to the floor, shot once, twice, three times, but the bullets went wild. Joan screamed and crouched on the steps, clutching Petey tightly. Knox and Orci bumped into a bench, overturning it.

The door crashed open, swinging on its hinges and the two plain-clothes men ran down the aisle toward the fighting Knox and Orci. Knox grabbed Orci's wrist, twisting it. Orci yelled with pain and dropped the gun.

Dawson held his over the two men. "Okay, Taylor, get out of the way."

Knox jumped up. "It's all right, Joan."

Orci, his clothes rumpled, his hat knocked off, lay on the floor, looking straight into the gun. Best leaned down and slipped the handcuffs on Orci's wrists.

"I'll beat this rap yet," Orci screamed.

Best gave the handcuffs a jerk and dragged Orci to his feet.

Dawson stepped toward Joan. "Are you all right, Mrs. Taylor?"

She stood up weakly and half-whispered, "I'm all right." *With a gun he was stronger than all of us, but now how weak and sniveling he is with a couple of detectives beside him.* "We're safe, Petey, dear, we're safe." She rocked the baby until he stopped crying.

"Let's go," Dawson said, starting down the aisle with Orci between him and Best.

"I'll be right back, Honey," Knox called, as he followed the men onto the porch. Joan could hear them talking. Petey dozed. Her fears crystallized into one big need. *Knox has got to take Petey and me away from here.*

Knox came in and strode toward her. "Honey, you were a winner!"

"I didn't feel like one. I was scared to death."

He dropped onto the stairs and put his arm around her.

"Knox, you will take us away, tonight?"

"Perhaps you would like to spend a few days with your mother?"

"No, I mean leave it all. Doesn't this prove to you that your work is dangerous? That you've got to make a real home for Petey and me?"

"Honey, you're upset! You see that Dawson and Best came out even when I told them not to. We're safe."

"I'm not going through another night like this!"

"You won't have to. It won't happen again."

"As long as you're in this kind of work, you don't know what is going to happen. I've been through enough. Either you quit this work or I'm going home to my mother."

"Joan, you wouldn't!"

"Yes I would. I mean it."

"But what about me?"

"If you love me and Petey you'll come, too. Dad will give you a job, I know he will, and we can live with my parents until you're established."

"Joan, you wouldn't ask me to do that."

"Yes, I would. I am." Desperate, she hunted in her mind for some argument to persuade him to do what she knew was right. And she thought of Vince. "Do you want Petey to turn from God, like Vince, because his father neglected him?"

"I'm sure Vince's father didn't mean to neglect him. He was just absorbed in his work."

"Too absorbed. Like you! But I'm not going to let you treat Petey that way. I'm going home and you can come with us, or —" She was so afraid he wouldn't agree that she couldn't continue.

Knox looked crushed as he said, "I have no choice! Phone your dad and if he'll give me a job I'll take it."

Joan went to the phone to call her mother. She had won, but there was no joy in her victory. Knox would go with her but his heart would remain here in the Valley with the boys.

PART III

KNOX   "He for God only, she for God in him."

Milton

1

"Wives, like children, need to be loved most when they least deserve it."

Dr. Paul Popenoe

Florence greeted Knox, Joan and Petey with an air of, "I might have known it would come to this" and had them moved into the guest suite of powder room, bath and bedroom. Pete cordially gave Knox a job that amounted to being official flunky. Knox disliked having superficial authority over something he didn't understand and asked to be transferred to the labor gang. Pete understandingly agreed, so Knox began shoving gravel into the cement mixer.

The hard labor kept him so tired that much of the time he felt numb. The only comfort he had in the situation was that Joan was apparently happy. She had lost her tense look and was constantly reminding him how beautiful the guest room was . . . wall to wall rose-colored shag rugs . . . cherry tree wallpaper . . . white TV set, ruffled pink spread on the low hollywood bed . . . peony pink drapes.

Each day, when he came home from work, at the lanai door, he took off his shoes so he wouldn't soil Florence's light green rugs. He walked through the gold and green hall, through the purple and gold powder room, into the bathroom. He had to bathe before he dared go into the beruffled pink bedroom.

Then, clean, all but his nails, under which the gray cement always stuck, he went into the bedroom. Joan, in a peppermint-striped frock, looked as appealing as ever. He kissed her, then flung himself down beside Petey, on the big bed.

143

"Tired?" Joan asked, sitting on the edge of the bed.

"Sure."

"Then, silly, why do you work with the foundation gang? Dad can hire a dozen men to mix concrete. You should have stayed in the office, and learned the business."

"I don't fit into contracting."

"How can you be so stubborn!"

He looked at her, her pink mouth set. *Who calls who stubborn?* "It's not my type of work."

"You could make it the right kind of work. There's money in building. And we go to church regularly, don't we? And you could be an elder. I wouldn't stop you from doing anything you want to for the Lord."

"Except serving Him full time?"

"Don't you like having a pretty home?"

"I like being with you and Petey."

"But you're not happy!"

"How can I be?"

"I'd think a man would be happy to see his wife and son well taken care of."

"Men are queer, Honey. We want to take care of our family in our own way."

"Even at the sacrifice of your own?"

"That seems to be the way it is."

He stared at her, so desirable and yet so remote.

The musical tones of a gong floated into the room. It was the warning bell that dinner was nearly ready. Joan picked up Petey and carried him into the dining room, to give him his bottle. Knox, not wanting to be in the same room with Florence any longer than necessary, deliberately waited until the second gong rang.

The dining room, with its floor covering of black, blue and pink diamonds, gray plastic table, with pink mats and turquoise dishes, gave Knox the feeling that he was dining in a section of a Better Homes Exhibit.

Dinner slipped by with little comment until Hortense, the VandenBerg's all-around servant, served chocolate pie with whipped-cream. Sharon looked at it and sighed, "Not for me!"

"Take it away, Hortense. Sharon must watch her figure," Florence ordered.

"Ain't no figure worth giving up pie! You're going to lose it some day anyway, and you might as well lose it the happy way."

"Not tonight," Sharon said. "I have a date with Vince."

"He phoned you?" Florence asked.

"At the office. He said he'll be here at seven-thirty."

"It's only right for you to go out with Vince," Florence continued. "He's a positively splendid young man. Has an excellent position, earns an excellent salary, and will amount to something someday. I'd be happy to have one of my daughters have sense enough to marry an excellent young man like him."

Knox flushed. In the month he had been at the Vanden-Berg's Florence never missed an opportunity to insult him.

"I wouldn't say that," Pete warned.

"I can speak my mind in my own home," Florence retorted.

Knox stalked out of the dining room, into the powder room.

Joan came into the room and put her soft hand on his shoulder. "Don't mind Mom."

"Nearly every mealtime she manages to insult me."

"She always did make mealtime a sort of platform. It's the one time we're all together."

"There's too much I don't understand. I think I'll go see Aunt Bea," he said desperate.

"I wish you wouldn't."

"It's only fair to her." When they had moved, he had been too upset to face Aunt Bea, but had sent a note and keys by Vince.

Joan gave him a hurt look and flounced into the bedroom.

Perhaps Aunt Bea can tell me why, when I thought I was in the Lord's will, everything went so wrong.

He made an appointment to see Aunt Bea the following Thursday evening. It made him hopeful even to be with her again in her office. He wanted to talk of himself, but didn't know how to begin, so he asked, "How's Leon?"

"You'd be pleased. He comes to Grace Church faithfully, has a job and is trying to persuade Mickey to marry him."

"And the other boys?"

"Leon keeps in touch with them. Wes pilfered from the grocery store where he was working and was put on probation. Topper's joined a choral group. But Duke and Tom joined the gang that tried to break into the house Halloween."

"And Homer?"

"He was out of the hospital ten days, but had no one to help him so he went back on heroin, was arrested and sent back to the hospital."

"Poor kid! And Billie?"

"She's married."

"Perhaps that's best. And Gail?"

"I haven't heard a word about her for a long time. And you?"

He couldn't avoid the issue any longer. "You know I'm not happy."

"I tried to warn you that night at Mountain Top. I've seen this happen too often. The man wants to serve God, regardless of the cost. The girl wants ruffled curtains and an electric mixer. Good things, but sometimes getting them costs the man time he'd spend helping others."

He strode to the rear of the room, paused at the grand piano and stared up at the picture of Christ. Then he came back. "I don't want to go on like this."

"Yet, if you force Joan to go back with you, it will only end as it did before."

He remembered when he had been working on his shotput and could make only fifty-six inches. Month after month he couldn't budge that mark, then one day he made fifty-seven, five. "When I see my way out, I'll phone you."

"I'll always be delighted to help."

He went back to watching Joan look lovely but set, to little Petey cooing in his crib, to letting Florence sandpaper his nerves.

Two slow dreary months went by before Hortense showed two guests into the powder room. The slightly built Leon, wearing a cheap, neat brown suit, had grown into a serious young man. And Mickey had become a young lady with trim bobbed hair, a smoldering look in her brown eyes, wearing a yellow sweater and brown checked skirt.

"Hi, Champ," Leon said.

"It's good to see you!" Knox answered, pleased that the couple thought enough of him to look him up.

"Both of you," Joan agreed.

"Aunt Bea told me where to find you."

Knox waved his hand toward the settee. Leon sat down gawking at the frilly room. Mickey sat beside him, treating the room with mild boredom, as if she were used to much, much better.

Joan dropped onto the chair in front of the dressing table, with the mirror reflecting her upswept curls and slim, rounded shoulders. Knox sat on a spindle-legged chair, balancing carefully so it wouldn't break. "How are your folks?"

"Them adult delinquents? I'll convert them yet. I got Mom to go to church with me. The Old Man, he's still gotta sleep. But Mickey and me, we come special to tell you a hunk of news."

"What's up?"

"I'm taking a chance on the brute," Mickey smiled fondly at Leon.

Knox grinned at the idea of anyone calling Leon a brute. "You're both young."

"Not so very! I'm eighteen and got a job."

"Mom will sign the license, tickled to get rid of me. She's got her hands full again."

"What's wrong?"

"Dad! He don't know how to make nothing but trouble. He's made parole, but he ain't keeping it. Seems like he can't. He don't know nothing but the wrong kind of friends. Mom is worried stiff that he'll be picked up and she'll be dragged through the papers again, but she's too drooly about him to leave."

"I'm sorry," Joan said.

"Leon had better not act up, for I'm not going to take what Mom has."

"I tell you a million times, you don't need to worry about me." Leon faced Knox. "I'll never get over knowing you and all that you did for us fellows. I wasn't caring nothin' about what happened to me. Then I met you and I saw that I could trust you, that you cared! Something my folks never did. Then you told me about the Lord and I believed in Him. And I'm not going to do things that would make Mickey unhappy because I'm not going to do them — period!"

Leon's my proof that I was doing right.

"I've told my dad about you, lots. I wish he could meet you. You might be able to help him," Mickey said.

Florence came out of the bedroom, where she had been looking after Petey. Knox jumped to his feet and introduced her.

"Pleased to meet you," Leon said. "We were just saying what a great work Champ did in the Valley. Why don't you come back? The joint stands there. And this time the kids didn't bust the windows. They're hoping you'll come back!"

"I should hope Knox knows better than to return there after his fiasco!" Florence set her chin and left the room.

"The fellows need you."

The palms of Knox's hands sweated. He ached to go back. "It's up to Joan!"

"Didn't you like it there?" Mickey pleaded. "We all loved Petey and did what we could to help."

"I know you did, but you see, we're really more comfortable here," Joan answered.

Mickey glanced at the violet shepherd and shepherdess on the dressing table. "I suppose it would be nice to have a first-class joint like this. Natch, Leon and I will have to start small. But I tell you this much, we're having a place of our own, and ain't telling my old man where it is, or Mom either! I don't want to get dragged into them papers again."

"When are you being married?" Joan asked.

"Saturday night, after I get through work, so we'll have Sunday for a honeymoon," Leon answered.

"Leon and I went to Olvera House and Mr. Buchanan is marrying us. I met a first-class lady there, who's going to decorate the place swell for the wedding. She was married there once, but she's a widow now."

"What's her name?" Joan asked, with sudden interest.

"Alison Moore. She's really pretty."

"So she's back in town! And you knew it, didn't you?" Joan sprang to her feet and stared at Knox.

"I didn't," he said, surprised at the news.

Joan darted by him into their room, slamming the door.

"I'm sorry Joan's upset. I used to go around with Alison before I met Joan, and she doesn't like her," Knox tried to explain.

"I can understand that," Mickey nodded.

"But it don't make things so hot, does it?" Leon said.

"Not too much, but I can't go back to the Valley until I'm sure Joan wants to go."

"Meanwhile, you, the Champ, live here," Leon waved his hand at the ornate room.

"And with your mother-in-law, too. Looks to me that she'd be something like Gram to live with."

"We get along."

"Because Champ keeps his mouth shut," Leon said. "Come on, Mickey, let's get going. We'll be seeing you at the wedding."

"I'll see."

Knox walked with them to their car, and then bracing himself, he went into the bedroom. Petey was asleep in his crib. Joan, her eyes puffy from crying, was lying on the bed. Knox stood over her. She looked slight and appealing. "Honey, haven't I proved that I love you? Forget Alison and think of the other things that Leon told me, of the fellows' need for someone to care, to know about the Lord."

"How can you ever want to go back there and sacrifice little Petey?"

"Don't you give me credit for learning anything? I know I've got to find a balance between my work and my family, and if you'll help me, I think I can find it."

"This home is good enough for me, and we're not going to Mickey's and Leon's wedding!"

"Why?"

"If you go I'll consider it only an excuse to see Alison."

"But Leon and Mickey will be disappointed."

"I don't care!"

There's no use arguing with Joan. But into his heart came the errant thought that if he were married to Alison, he could serve the Lord as he so greatly desired.

2

"A news sense is really a sense of what is important, what is vital, what has color and life — what people are interested in."

Burton Rascoe

Home from work, a few days later, Knox cleaned up and hopefully thought, *Now for a peaceful hour before I have to face Florence.* He crossed the powder room into the bedroom, and there Florence was sitting on an easy chair and Joan on the white hassock in front of TV. Surprised, Knox wondered, *What's Florence doing in our room this time of day? Usually she's fussing with Hortense about dinner.*

Joan nodded for him to come closer. He picked up Petey from the crib and crossed to Joan's side. She whispered, "It's some man, threatening to jump."

Knox, holding Petey, crouched on the floor and stared at the twenty-four inch screen. Joan was tuned to a channel that specialized in wrestling, westerns and local events. Knox listened to the announcer until he realized that he was looking at Hill Street, in front of the Los Angeles Hall of Justice. The daylight savings provided enough light at five p.m. for the telecast.

Seemingly hundreds of people were staring upward. Lieutenant Dawson and Inspector Best were standing by a car, talking over a hand microphone. The camera angle shifted, the telescopic lens picking up a man, his arms outstretched, balancing himself on the ornamental ledge around the tenth floor of the Hall of Justice.

"He's a prisoner," Joan went on. "He escaped somehow

150

and got out on that ledge. He says he'll jump if the police don't make a deal with him. Says he has nothing to live for."

"How long has he been there?"

"I don't know. Since about three-thirty, I think. Anyway, around four the announcer broke in, saying the station would bring us a public service feature, and switched to this man."

"What length they won't go to get listeners!"

"It pays!" Florence spoke up. "Don't you remember that Kathy Fiscus rescue, Joan? Your father watched it at a neighbor's and the next day he bought a TV set."

Knox stared at the slight figure of a man perched so high above the street. "Why don't they go out and get him?"

"He says if anyone comes out on the ledge, he'll jump and they'll both go down."

"I don't see how they hear what he says."

"See that black thing dangling there? The police dropped a microphone over the roof so he can talk to them."

"I see."

The camera panned the long way down from the man on the ledge to the ground, where police were spreading a net to catch the would-be suicide if he jumped. People watched, their necks craned upward. Some of them shouted at the man. Dawson was talking into the microphone. "O'Brien, you know we won't bargain. You've got too many counts against you. But what do you gain by jumping? If you come back in, we'll be fair, and the time will come when you'll be back with your wife and Mickey."

"Mickey!" Knox almost shouted. "Don't you know who's on that ledge? That's Speedy O'Brien, Mickey's father."

"Do you think so?"

"She said he was back in jail, and that's a man named O'Brien, with a daughter, Mickey."

"She said he was running with the wrong crowd, not that he was in jail."

He didn't answer. *She told me at her wedding and Joan mustn't know I went.* He had stopped by Olvera House on his way to Santa Ana to visit his parents. He had admired Alison's courage and faith, but Mickey had been the center of interest. Afterwards he had driven her and Leon to their new home.

The camera switched again to O'Brien. He was straining to talk into the swinging microphone. "Don't give me that! I'm going to jump. It's all that's left for me, but you always grant a dying man's last wish, and I want to see my girl. I want to say good-by to her. She's all I love in the world."

"Okay, where does she live?" said Dawson.

"I don't know. She married some punk named Leon Nye a couple of weeks ago and hasn't been to see me since. I've lost her. I ain't got no reason to live."

"We'll get her for you, but how are we going to find out where she lives?"

"You're cops, ain't you? That's your business!"

The camera switched to the street level. A woman had come up to Dawson. He stopped talking, and the announcer began recapping the events. The camera focused on the young woman. Knox recognized Alison! *Why not, Olvera House is close by and she has heard th*at *O'Brien is the man on the ledge.*

"What's up?" Pete asked, coming into the room. Florence held up her hand to silence him. He dropped onto the white chest at the foot of the bed and turned the knob of his hearing aid. Sharon came in, tossed her gloves, hat and jacket on the bed and sat beside her father. Hortense followed her and announced, "Dinner is ready. I rang the gong twice and no one comes."

"Hortense, a criminal is posed on the Hall of Justice, demanding to see his daughter and until he does, Los Angeles is too entertained to eat," Pete explained.

On the screen, Dawson turned to the microphones. "Do you hear me, O'Brien? We have a worker here from Olvera House. She says she was at your daughter's wedding and though she doesn't know where Mickey lives, she knows the man who took her and her husband home after the wedding. We're going to trace your daughter through him. Give me your word that you'll not jump until I get back with Mickey."

Me! Knox's face drained. *I'll have to admit I was at the wedding for O'Brien's sake. What will Joan think?*

"She doesn't know where this man lives but believes she can locate him through the phone book," Dawson continued.

"Who are you looking for?" the announcer broke in.

"Knox Taylor, Olympic decathlon champion."

"You!" Joan exclaimed. "You went to the wedding!"

"Sure, I went."

"You promised you wouldn't."

"I didn't."

"You went to see Alison."

"I wouldn't say that," Pete's gentle voice warned.

"I don't know what else you expected of him," Florence slurred.

"Perhaps I could help as referee," Sharon volunteered.

Knox ignored them, persisting, "I saw Alison only casually. I couldn't disappoint Leon and Mickey."

"You think more of them than you do me, and always have!"

Petey began to whimper. Joan took him from Knox and hurried out of the room.

"Don't you all want to eat?" Hortense asked. "The dinner's gonna get all dried out."

"Serve dinner in here on trays," Florence decided.

"I'll help," Sharon stood up. "Only, Dad, don't let me miss anything." She followed Hortense out of the room.

"What'll I do?" Knox turned to Pete.

"You'd better wait until the police contact you," Pete decided.

"You're right." He dropped into Joan's chair. *If only I could talk to Joan. But it's no use when she's upset.*

The camera picked up the announcer, a young man with a confident manner. He recapped what had happened, telling that Dawson and Alison Moore had gone to find Knox Taylor, who had taken Mickey O'Brien Nye home from her wedding. He also pleaded for Mickey, if she were listening, to get in touch with the police department at once, so they could bring her to her father. Then he turned to the crowd and began asking bystanders what they would do to get the man off the ledge.

"Let him jump. This is a free country," said a surly man.

"Have Roy Rogers lasso him from the roof," said a youngster.

"Send a policeman out to arrest him and he'll have to come in," said a young girl.

"Get more nets, only higher up," said a man in working clothes.

"Get the man's mother. She'll plead with him," said an older woman.

The phone rang shrilly. Knox jumped up and answered. "Knox Taylor speaking." Florence and Pete stood behind him, listening. Sharon and Hortense hurried into the room.

"Hi, Knox, this is your old friend, Dawson. Got your TV set turned on?"

"Sure."

"Then you know what's up. Do you know where this Mickey O'Brien Nye lives?"

"Sure."

"Does she have a phone?"

"I don't think so. She and Leon wanted to get away from her father."

"What's the address?"

"It's on Whitmore Place, but I don't remember the number as I was there only once."

"Could you go back to it?"

"Sure."

"Then we'll be out for you. It won't take us long, with the sirens going, but you be at your door. That crazy O'Brien might take a notion to jump."

"I'll be ready." Knox put the phone back on its stand. He explained to the family, adding, "I've got to show Dawson where Mickey and Leon live."

"You'd better have your dinner first."

"I'll eat on the porch, what I can." Knox got a sports jacket out the closet, then stalked out of the room. In the hall, he glanced into the dining room. Joan, seated in one of the lowslung modern chairs, was holding the gurgling Petey in her arms. With a tender smile on her heart-shaped face, she looked like a modern madonna. Knox felt anew his need of her understanding and stepped to the doorway, gripping the jamb with his hand. In a low, pleading tone he said, "I've got to take Mickey to her father. He needs her."

"All right," she answered, poking gooey spinach into Petey's mouth.

She thinks she's staying here for him, but she's ruining my life. He went out onto the porch.

Pete joined him. "I suppose we'll hear the sirens."

"Sure, we'll hear them."

Hortense came out with a tray. "You'd better eat this. The roast beef is good. And I'll be watching you on TV."

"I won't be on TV," Knox said. He dropped onto one of the porch chairs and began eating in hurried bites.

From a distance he heard the mounting cry of the sirens. He put down his fork, and with Pete walked to the edge of the sidewalk. The siren grew louder and louder. Neighbors looked out of the windows or came out on their lawns. The police car swung around and stopped. Dawson jumped out and opened the door to the back seat. Pete slapped Knox on the back, "You'll win this time."

With a quick, "Hello," to Dawson, Knox jumped into the back seat, only to see Alison there. Again he said, "Oh, hello."

Dawson slid in front with Best, and with the siren on full blast, Best whirled around and started back down the street. Dawson spoke into the two-way radio, "Tell O'Brien that we've got Taylor and that we're on our way to his daughter's place."

With an anxious expression on her oval face, Alison said, "I hope I didn't cause any trouble, Knox, but I didn't know what else to do."

"It was all you could do!" But Knox could picture Joan at the TV listening to the announcer report that he was in the car with Dawson, Best and Alison Moore.

Best swung onto the freeway into the fast lane. Dawson turned halfway around in his seat and explained, "O'Brien has been nothing but a moody trouble-maker for years. He loves to play to a crowd. I doubt if he intends to jump, though with his record he hasn't much to lose. He broke parole, held up a bank, and might have got away with it, but he beat up his wife."

"I don't remember Mickey ever saying that he beat her mother," Knox said, troubled.

"He doesn't usually, but he says his mother-in-law drove him to it. He can't stand her nagging, and she made so much trouble between him and his wife that he beat her up and went on a bender. When O'Brien started a fight at a bar, a bartender called the cop. In the lineup we got a partial identification. It's difficult to get a proper identification when a man has a handkerchief over his face, but he's the same build and has a record for armed robbery. We found a gun in the O'Brien apartment. And his mother-in-law will swear that he wasn't home at the time of the holdup. So far he hasn't come up with an alibi."

As the car approached downtown, they swung around the clover leaf, heading toward Hollywood. Best had his red light flashing and it was amazing the way cars cleared over to the third lane to get out of the way of the police car. They were making time!

"I'm glad you could come, Knox," Alison said. "You know how Mickey hates being in the papers, but she and Leon will do anything you say. When I listened to them tell of the work you did in the Valley, I wish you could go back there."

He set his chin. *This evening will probably make Joan more determined than ever not to go back. She'd think that I'd be thrown in with Alison.*

They sped by several ramps, then Best swung off the Gower Street turn-off, toward the hills. On Whitmore Place, Knox recognized the house. Best parked while Knox and Dawson went to the little apartment built on the side of a hillside home. Knox knocked.

Mickey opened the door. "Champ, come in! Leon isn't home yet. You know he works until after seven."

"Mickey, get your coat and come with us. Your father needs you."

"Dad's 'in' again?"

"He needs you. I'll tell you about it in the car."

"A police car?" She glanced at the solidly-built Dawson.

"Yes. This is my old friend, Lieutenant Dawson. I'm with them, Mickey. It's right for you to come."

"If you say so." She got her short jacket, walked with Knox and Dawson to the car. Dawson quickly introduced Best, and when she saw Alison, she smiled with relief. Best headed toward the freeway. Dawson bent forward, talking on the radio. "Tell O'Brien that we have his daughter and to hang on until we get there."

"What happened?" Mickey asked.

"Your father went to court today," Dawson explained, "and as you may know, there's a private elevator to take the prisoners from the courtroom to the jail. When the time came for Officer Hughes to take your father upstairs, he didn't handcuff him because there seemed to be no need.

"They got off at the tenth floor. The elevator man closed the door. Your father and Hughes were standing at the end of a narrow hall. Hughes turned toward the booking desk. But the window washers had been working. The grill on the window was open. Speedy was quick enough to see his chance. He swung on Hughes, knocking him down, then ran and climbed out the window onto the ledge. He wants to see you and promised not to jump until we get you there. And when we do, you've got to persuade him to come back in through that window."

"To prison? I don't know if I can or not." Mickey slumped back in her seat, her eyes big in her thin, worried face.

Knox pressed his strong hand over her limp one. "Pray, Mickey. Your father mustn't jump. He's not ready to go."

3

"The more any man is a servant to the Lord, the more is he a man of God to his fellow-men."

Charles John Ellicott

The second the police car drove off the Civic Center ramp, Best turned on the siren. A road block had been set up and the police were turning all cars north, but Best drove south on North Broadway.

Thick crowds seemed to be everywhere and the police had stretched ropes, keeping the throng away from the net and television operating unit. A sound truck, camera truck and a truck with powerful searchlights on it were parked along the west side of the street. Technicians, with head sets, were on both trucks and street. Thick wires snaked across Broadway. A huge heavy net was stretched in front of the Hall of Justice, almost blocking the entrance and filling half of the street. At the far end, policemen kept the traffic moving along Temple Street.

Best turned off the siren and parked the car. Dawson jumped out and went around to let Alison and Mickey out. Knox got out on the street side, walked around, and as he stood beside Dawson and the girls, he was conscious that the TV camera, with its gleaming red light, was focused on them. *I'm on that screen at home, with Joan watching me. Perhaps even Mom and Dad can see me.*

"We've been relaying your messages to O'Brien, but I think he enjoys having everyone pay attention to him," a plain-clothes man told Dawson, passing a hand mike to him.

"O'Brien." Dawson raised the mike to his mouth. "Can you hear me?"

"I can hear you. Let's see what you cops produced."

Knox looked up to where O'Brien's amplified voice came from. He was but a black blot against the side of the white building.

"We've got your daughter, Mickey, here," Dawson's voice boomed.

"Then let's hear her. I've been waiting long enough and I'm about ready to take the big dive," came the whine of O'Brien's weary voice.

Mickey stepped up to the microphone. "Dad, it's me! Mickey!"

Knox stepped beside her and put his hand on her shoulder. People around whispered. Knox frowned at them but they kept on talking to one another, and in the distance the traffic continued to hum.

"Mickey, little girl, I'm doing you the biggest favor I ever did. I'm taking myself out of your way. You won't have to be ashamed of your dad any more. You can remember him as the man who gave his life for you."

"No, Dad, don't. You know Mom and I love you."

"You don't love me or you wouldn't have run away and married that punk without telling me where you were going."

"It was that we didn't want to be in the papers."

"You're in them now, but this is the last time. I won't live to drag your precious name into the papers again."

"Dad, you're not ready to die."

"How do I know there's any life after death? I want to end it all."

"But you must believe what Jesus said, 'In my Father's house are many mansions,' and that proves there is life after death."

"I'll take a chance!"

"You've taken a chance on a lot of things and didn't get by with them, any more than you'll get by with dying."

"How come you know so much?"

"It's that Knox Taylor I've been telling you about. He told me about the Lord Jesus and believing in Him has made life different for Leon and me, and it can for you, too!"

"Not for me! I'm too old. I've ruined my life."

"I can't explain it all to you. Will you talk to Knox? He's here. He's the one who found me for you."

"Put him on. I need someone to bless my dying moments."

Mickey passed the microphone to Knox. Alison moved next to Knox and put her arm around Mickey.

"Can you hear me?" Knox called.

"Better than I did Mickey."

"Then listen. She's right. Christ can give you something to live for. It's never too late for a man to turn to Him."

"You ask Dawson and he'll tell you that I've got too many years facing me. I'll never get out again."

"You can live for God in prison."

"Who wants to? You're a fine one, suggesting that, when you're walking around, doing what you please!"

Mickey grabbed the microphone from Knox's hand. "If I prove to you that Knox doesn't do what he pleases and yet lives for God, will you believe what he says and get off that ledge?"

O'Brien didn't answer. Everyone in the crowd stared at him. Mickey continued, "You've complained that you couldn't live right because you didn't have the breaks. But neither has the Champ."

"Go ahead and prove to me that this sprinter is a man of God!"

"Even though he was a champion, nowadays he works mixing cement. That's plenty hard, isn't it? Harder than you've ever worked."

"What does that prove?"

"It proves that he doesn't just preach. But it's more than that. You think any man could live with Gram and be a man of God?"

"She's made a devil out of me and would out of any man."

"Knox has a mother-in-law who's like Gram. And he lives with her in peace."

A cold chill passed through Knox at the thought of Florence sitting at the TV in Joan's room, hearing what Mickey had said! Alison put her hand comfortingly on his arm.

"Any man who can live with his mother-in-law in peace is a right man to me. I'll come in and talk to him."

A cheer went up from the crowd. O'Brien began edging toward the window. A camera swung onto Knox and the announcer said, "Taylor, you've won again! You got that man to face life when no one else could. Tell us, is this the greatest thrill of your life?"

Knox hesitated. *How easy it would be to say "yes"!* Instead he answered, "The greatest thrill was the day I gave my life to God, from my track shoelaces to my dreams." *And He took them both!!*

"He's safe." Mickey began to sob and clung to Knox.

He patted her shoulder and looked up. The black blot that had been O'Brien was gone.

"The men have him up there," Dawson said, "but I'll take you and Mickey up to see him."

Mickey turned to Alison and begged, "Come with me."

"Of course."

The men edged the net back so that Dawson, Mickey and Alison could get by. The crowd surged forward. A man reached out and shook Knox's hand, "Great work, Reverend." Someone else called, "Still the same old champ." He waved at them, thankful for their friendliness. Then he walked up the wide steps and into the Hall of Justice. The door closed behind him. Relief filled him. *I'm out of camera range. Florence and Joan can't see me any longer.*

They went up in the elevator to the men's section of the jail, into the glass-enclosed visitors' room.

O'Brien was sitting behind a long table with a wooden partition in the center of it, reaching the middle of his chest. There were deep circles under his eyes, his hair was uncombed, and he was handcuffed to a guard sitting beside him.

"Dad!" Mickey ran to the table, leaned over and kissed him.

Mickey sat on a stool between Alison and Knox. Dawson stood behind them. And Mickey said, "Don't do that again! Don't you know Mom and I love you?"

"Maybe. Anyway, I did some thinking while I waited for you to get here. I know I've thrown my life away. Do you think there's hope for me?"

"I know it," Knox spoke up.

O'Brien looked at Dawson. "I thought I was to get to talk to Champ alone."

"Okay," Dawson nodded to the guard. He unlocked the handcuffs and he, Dawson, Alison and Mickey went to the other side of the glass partition.

Alone with Knox, O'Brien said, "Is what Mickey says true? That you live a holy life with the breaks against you?"

"I don't live a holy life, but I don't go in for breaking the law, either legal or moral, if that's what you mean."

O'Brien sunk lower in his chair, "I guess that's what I mean. With the breaks against you, do you manage to keep it straight?"

Knox instinctively glanced at Alison, knowing how it would be to have a wife in sympathy with his plans for his life. But with steady resolve, he said, "I run it straight."

"Then shoot the works. I'll listen."

Knox breathed a silent prayer. *How does one talk about the Lord to a man who has spent his life in crime?* He began, "In a sense, life is like a race, only all men can win, if they will. The goal is heaven. Like any race it takes commitment and training to win. When you mess around like you have, then you're breaking the rules and fouling up everything."

"That ain't no lie!"

"Any sprinter will tell you that he owes much to his coach. And we have a Coach in this race of life, the Lord Jesus. All you need to win is to believe in Him as Saviour and follow Him."

"But an old broken-down wreck like me — would God want me?"

"The apostle Paul said, 'Christ Jesus came into the world to save sinners, of whom I am chief.' If he was chief, then the rest of us have a chance."

"If I turn to God, will He get me out of jail?"

"He might, but probably He won't. You see, being a Christian isn't putting a prayer in a slot and having the answer you want come out. Being a Christian is a relationship to God that enables you to live above circumstances . . . be it a concentration camp, a sick bed, an unappreciative wife." *I'm sorry that slipped in.* "Or prison." And then, he patiently explained the best he could what it meant to believe in the Lord Jesus as Saviour and to live for Him. The minutes ticked away. Dawson paced back and forth. The guard kept his eyes glued on O'Brien. Knox kept on talking until O'Brien said, "I'll go for anything once."

"Then pray."

"On my knees?"

"No, just bow your head and tell the Lord all about it."

"I ain't much on praying."

"It's talking to God, that's all."

O'Brien bowed his head, began mumbling and crying. Knox bowed his own head and prayed silently, *Lord, do use me! I've got to go back to that Valley and work for You. If Joan understands or not. Help me.*

O'Brien lifted his face, with tears running down the wrinkles. Knox passed him a handkerchief and nodded to Dawson. The officers came into the room and O'Brien said, "You guys ain't going to have no more trouble with me."

"It's about time," the guard said and slipped the handcuffs back on O'Brien.

Mickey and Alison came in and Mickey explained, "I phoned a neighbor to go tell Leon what had happened, but she'd seen me on TV. I guess everyone in Los Angeles has seen me. But it's first-class with Dad safe."

They talked a little longer with O'Brien, then the guard led him back to his cell and Dawson took the three visitors down in the elevator, to the main floor. A lone reporter was waiting in the corridor. He began asking Knox and Mickey questions. They told him about O'Brien's decision to live for God in prison. The reporter eyed Knox, "Are you a minister?"

"No, but I used to be a boys' worker out in the Valley."

"Out in the Valley, huh?"

"Yes, I'm going back there."

"When did you decide that?"

"When I was talking to O'Brien."

"Champ is first-class with boys." Mickey began telling the reporter about the work Knox had done in the Valley.

This will be in the papers tomorrow. If no one else is happy, at least Gramps will be.

"Come on," Dawson said, hustling Knox, Alison and Mickey

out to the street. "I'll take the girls home and I've asked Sergeant Malone to take you home, Knox. Thanks for helping us with O'Brien."

"Leon and I will be with you as soon as you and Joan move back to the Valley," Mickey smiled.

"Thanks."

She and Dawson walked to the parked car where Best was waiting. Knox glanced up and down the street. The crowd had thronged it an hour ago, but now it was nearly deserted. A gust of wind blew a piece of newspaper down the street. He looked at Alison. Her blue eyes glowed. She said, "I'm glad you're going back to working with boys. Will Joan be willing?"

"I don't know."

"If you do go into boys' work, I'll probably see you from time to time."

He nodded.

"What will Joan say to that?"

"I don't know. I do know I love her and want to work out our marriage."

"Knox, you and Ben have both died for what you believe. He the quick way, you the slow!"

"Thanks," *It is good to have Alison's respect. But Lord, I need Joan's understanding.*

4

"Mutual love, the crown of all our bliss."
Milton

Knox got out of the police car, said good night to Sergeant Malone, and with reluctant feet walked up the pathway to the VandenBerg house. Every light seemed on. Even Hortense was still busy in the kitchen.

He walked into the gaudy powder room where he had prayed so many mornings and paused. *I'd rather face ten thousand decathlon champions than Florence. Only she challenges me to the right to be with my wife and son.* He could hear excited voices beyond the door and knew that they were waiting for him.

He opened the door. Florence, a white chenille robe covering her portly figure, was pacing the floor. She stopped and glared at him. Sharon, seated on the cedar chest, was carefully filing her nails. Pete, still in his working clothes, stood behind Joan. In her rose-flecked robe, Joan was sitting in an easy chair, holding the sleeping Petey. The TV set had been turned off.

"Hi, Hero!" Sharon gave him a friendly smile. "Joanie, let me take Petey out and give him a bottle or something. I'd hate to have him see Champ meet his match."

"Will you, Sis?" Joan passed Petey to her sister.

"Leave it all to me." She hugged the baby and carried him out of the room.

"How dare you set foot in my home after you publicly disgraced me?" Florence raged.

"I wouldn't say that, Flo. It wasn't Knox but that girl who said things against you." Pete put his hand on Florence's arm as if to restrain her.

165

"I'm leaving tonight, so don't worry about me." Knox walked to the closet, took out his suitcase and flung it on the bed.

"I was never so humiliated in my life. After all we've done for you, taking you in when you couldn't make a living. I tell you the entire family will be glad to get rid of you, for once and for all. Joanie's father will pay for her divorce. The quicker she can be rid of you, the better."

Joan jumped up, crossed in front of Knox and faced her mother. "Leave Knox alone! He is a man of God!"

"Joan!" Knox gasped.

"That miserable failure! If he were a man of God, God would bless him."

"Please try to understand. I've lived with Knox. I know him. And if a man prays as Knox does, and says he's guided of God, we've got to believe him."

Knox sought Joan's slim hand and squeezed it, thankful for her confidence.

"You have to respect a person's right to do what he thinks God would have him," Pete defended.

"Are you all against me? Me . . . who has been pictured to the world as a shrew?"

"Mickey was desperate, trying to get her dad off that ledge," Knox excused, sorry for his mother-in-law.

"Flo, let Knox and Joan work it out."

"I never want to see either one of them again, or anyone else in the entire world." Florence began to cry. Pete put his arm about her gently and led her out of the room.

"Mom's deeply hurt, but you weren't to blame," Joan said.

"Honey, dare I hope that you'll come back with me? I'm going back to the Valley, to the fellows."

The phone rang. Knox glanced from it to Joan, and then picked it up. "Hello."

"Hi," came Vince's voice. "Saw your TV appearance tonight. It was the greatest broadcast of the year. Better than any spectacular."

"It was an all-time low."

"I imagine that Florence is plenty burnt up, but we'll all

work on her and bring her around. The news broadcaster said you're going back to the Valley to work with the delinks."

"That's for sure!"

"This time you can really go in style. That TV put you over. You'll find a hundred organizations and businessmen in the Valley back of you. And I'm offering to be on your board, treasurer, no less."

"Thanks. And I suppose you're right about the interest in my work. Maybe even Dad will be satisfied when he sees others accept me."

"How can he help it? This being a saint, it's tricky business, but you're making it."

"Thanks."

"Give me a ring in the morning and we'll get together."

Vince hung up. Knox turned to Joan. "That was Vince, offering to be treasurer of my work in the Valley. He says people will back me this time. But what I want to know is, Honey, are you going to back me?"

She walked back to the slipper chair by the silent TV, a slight figure with golden curls piled high on her head. She wiped her eyes with a small floral handkerchief. Wondering, he crossed to her side and knelt beside her. "Knox, I sat here and watched you on TV. You looked so clean and strong. Alison Moore was standing beside you. And I saw one thing special."

"What?"

"You don't love her," she said happily. "She put her hand on your arm and you didn't notice it. If you had loved her, you would have reacted differently."

"Thank God for TV, if it proved what I couldn't prove to you. Alison would be a good worker with me. We have many of the same interests, but even at your worst, I love you."

"I know, and what hurt me was that I saw her standing beside you when I knew I should have been there. I never have been with you as I should."

"Yes, you have. When we disagreed over the engagement ring, still you defended me. And tonight! And in the future, you always will be, won't you, Honey?"

"Yes."

He pulled her toward him and kissed her with fierce possession. Then he began walking up and down the room, outlining what they should do. "We'll stay here tonight. In the morning I'll phone Aunt Bea and Vince and we'll get together and make plans. Pete will understand and get someone else to do my work on the job, and —"

She laughed, "Silly, you give me five minutes and then, off you go!"